TEARS AND SCARS

By The Same Author

DUNGEON OF DESPAIR

TEARS AND SCARS

PENJENI MADZIKANGAVA

Harp Bookz International

An Imprint of TatendaCharlesMunyuki Publishing

TEARS AND SCARS

First published in Zimbabwe in 2016
Harp Bookz International
an imprint of Tatenda Charles Munyuki Publishing.

ISBN   978 0 7974 7253 2

Printed and bound by Harp Bookz International,
Harare, Zimbabwe.
harpbookz@gmail.com

facebook.com/tcmpublishingzim

CHAPTER 1

HARMONY

I vividly recall the day, for the day was no ordinary day. It was so special; it still has a compartment or rather an apartment in my heart. The day that I had been waiting for in bated breath had finally arrived. That day will remain entrenched in my memory bank.

It seems like yesterday and yet almost four decades have flirted by since that day dawned and dusked away. The journey that made the day no ordinary had been mooted by Amai three months back. She had shared her intention with Baba who did not object to the proposal.

Having secured the green light from Baba, Amai had to prepare for the journey. This journey was not ordinary just like the day. A lot of importance was attached to that day in 1975. Exactly four years later the nation broke the yoke of colonial bondage.

Amai and I were to travel to Salisbury the then capital city of Rhodesia. Blacks then affectionately referred to Salisbury as *Sobhaya*.

Those were the days of *Chilapalapa*, a language that had been devised by whites to enable them to communicate with illiterate blacks mostly those of Malawian and Zambian extraction. Then *Chibhende*, a form of language designed to tease and chide those who were not well versed with it, was also rife and rampant. It was a language that a group of youths could design so that it gave them leverage when they came into contact with those they perceived to be their nemesis.

Amai and I intended to visit Amainini Jekunareta who resided in Gillingham now Dzivarasekwa. I got so engrossed in the preparation of the journey to Salisbury that I forgot about the accommodation crisis that awaited us.

The houses then were too small to accommodate eight children. Luckily, for Amai and Amainini Jekunareta, Babamunini Gorobheki was a night sentinel, at a local school and spent most nights away from home.

Some of us, especially those who were young and naïve to bedroom politics, would be stashed away under a raised bed. The beds then were either made up of wood or spring and metal. Then people would angrily chide and mock those who would have crossed their paths by saying, '*Hindava uri rough semubhedha wemapuranga.*'

Then most couples preferred the springed and metalised beds, the ones that would always squeak and squawk as if in protest whenever somebody sat or slept on them. Those beds made a lot of unpleasant squeaking and squawking sounds that couples then would have to wait to enjoy their conjugal rights way after midnight.

You would hear wives, especially those who would have visited their husbands for their God given nocturnal rights admonishing their husbands, '*Baba Timoti, chimbomirai kani vana havasati varara, zvanyanyoita seiko nhai Sinyoro?*'

The husband, especially those who were faithful, yes those who would not stray out of their matrimonial home would try to convince their wives that indeed their children would have slept. But then wives being wives, would not throw caution to the wind and engage in acts that would impair their dignity.

Naughty children especially boys would feign to be asleep only to break into some naughty and muffled giggles whenever they felt their parents' harp of pleasure was serenading out of tune as they would be gasping for breath. I also forgot about a food crisis that also awaited us in Gillingham. Then most families could only afford two *decent* meals a day. In the morning, children would be served with sour porridge, *bota rehupfu hwakanyikwa or mutanda bota. Mutanda bota* was prepared with a syrup from *mauyu* fruits.

When the day finally dawned, Amai packed our clothes in a suitcase or *bhokisi* that had a draught or *tsoro* designed on top. She placed some sand boxes that would give the clothes an irresistible scent. The sand boxes that were usually white in colour, also waded off cockroaches that preyed and prowled on clothes.

When the day pandered to the whims of dusk, Baba who was struggling and trudging under the weight of the heavy suitcase that weighed him down heavily, led us to a bus stop in Fern Valley popularly known as *paFive Miles.*

Two sisters of mine who had been denied an opportunity by Baba to set their feet in Salisbury trailed us sobbing. A deluge of tears that threatened to wash away their dimples, cascaded in trickles of protests. I would be singing, '*Nhasi tiri kuvhaya, nhasi tiri kuvhaya.*'

Baba swiftly flagged down the first vehicle that came bearing down the tarmac. We later realised that the vehicle belonged to Baas Van de Burgh whose name a few blacks who lived in Fern Valley, then a white dominated community, had corrupted to *Vhandabhegi.*

As soon as we made ourselves comfortable in the spacious Zephyr Zodiac, the sleek machine took off as if it had been milling at a runway.

I felt sorry for my sisters who had broken into wails whilst clutching the back of their heads.

CHAPTER 2

RACIAL SEGREGATION

Baas Van de Burgh dropped us at the railway station. It was teeming with humanity. Baba joined a winding queue that snaked her way into the waiting room where blacks who would be issued with tickets waited for their turn to board the train.

Whites who travelled first class would be allowed into their coaches, which were as comfortable as they come. In there, they would snore their way to their destinations.

They would be served with some refreshments. Blacks who travelled in the economy coaches known as *mbombera*, would only be allowed to embark onto the train when the big and diesel powered millipede would be about to glide her way out of the station.

We would sing, '*Kushanja kune mangezi, kutsvaga chekufa ndicho,*' as the train hooted to signal her way out of the bay. Blacks believed that whites were daredevils who could dare and spoil for a fight with the devil.

We genuinely believed that whites could throw their fighting swords into the ring in a bid to square off with death. History tells us that whites then believed that once blacks were allowed into the coaches, they would start visiting the lavatory to answer calls of nature. The white establishment then argued that such an arrangement would leave the station littered with human excreta that would have dripped from lavatories.

As if that was not enough, coaches reserved for whites were just behind the diesel locomotives whilst those that housed blacks would always trail behind.

This was designed to segregate the two races. The two races should not have mixed to maintain the whites' aloofness. Deep in colonial Rhodesia, history tells us that whites looked upon anything black with disdain and yet would lick their plates dry after wolfing dishes prepared by black cooks.

They hated blacks to the footprint and yet would entrust black nannies with the welfare of their children. They would not trust blacks and as a result would make them travel at the back of a pickup or bakkie known then as half-tonne, whilst they cruised in the front in the company of their dogs.

But when the vehicle was to get involved in a fatal accident that would claim the life of the white guy behind the wheel sparing the black guy and the dog, white police officers would rush to record a warned and cautioned statement from the black guy. The black guy, who in most cases would have been travelling facing the opposite direction in a desperate bid to escape from the vagaries of the wind, instead of interrogating the dog that would have been privy to the goings on.

Legend has it that, whites would choose to confide in their pets than in a black man. History has it, that whites would choose to live a fortune in the hands or paws of their dogs and cats than blacks who would have taken care of them for the greatest part of their lives.

That was then, when whites would spend a fortune on a casket for their pets, just to give it a proper and decent burial whenever Mother Nature called them.

We enjoyed our travel in the brown economy coaches. The brown economy Rhodesian National Railways coaches would be teeming with humanity.

Serenity and tranquillity then prevailed in the coaches. Amai and I found seats on the brown coaches. I sat on the seat next to the window because I wanted to get a clearer picturesque view of the environment.

The seats were devoid of comfort. They were made of hardwood that left some gaps in between. Those were not seats, but rather benches that were pinned to the floor using bolts and nuts.

So big were the windows that they could allow any man to embark or disembark through them. The windows that had the acronym NRR, National Railways of Rhodesia emblazoned in gold at the centre, would only open by being lowered down.

There by the big window, I would watch the train panting, puffing, humming, groaning and writhing through the jungles that linked Umtali and Salisbury.

I could hear the groaning of the diesel engine powered millipede worming, navigating and manoeuvring her way through the dense forest of virgin land that harboured freedom fighters. So bright were the lights, as bright as the moonlight. The lights were as bright as tower lights that towered over houses in a plethora of African townships in Rhodesia.

Tower lights or rather floodlights that beamed and illuminated a myriad of stadia across African townships. Some tower lights then were adorned with speakers that spit spewed venom and propaganda that was billed onto us by the colonial establishment.

The messages of hate, of hopelessness, despair were phrased, laced, framed and packaged for the intended purpose of confusing some gullible blacks through propaganda that was rolled out like confetti at a wedding or with reckless abandon.

That was the colonial establishment for you, an establishment whose traits some gullible Africans died to ape, traits that had become so entrenched into the minds of some of our fellow blacks, blacks that had decided to become turncoats for a song.

For a song because no amount of money could buy the progressive thinking of some nationalist leaders who were there in the trenches executing and prosecuting the liberation struggle. No amount of money could change the black pigment of the colour black. No amount of parroting whites could make some blacks one of their own.

No bootlicking or rather wheedling could make blacks equal partners with whites in Rhodesia, which was under siege from flames of freedom. No amount of praise, worshipping whites could change the perception of whites towards blacks.

We remained sleeping partners in an establishment in which we were supposed to have been in the forefront making a dash for freedom.

We were supposed to be torchbearers in an establishment that had taken away those rights from us and forced on us inferiority complex, a complex that saw some among us grovelling, wobbling, quaking and shaking involuntarily in the presence of whites.

All this we were told at the bases by *vana Bhudhi Mukoma*. There during *pungwes,* freedom fighters would tell us that once the country attained her independence from colonial masters, all Zimbabweans would be equal.

Blacks would be able to employ whites as cooks, garden boys and nannies. Whites would relocate to the servants' quarters, whilst blacks would occupy the main houses in the leafy Eastern suburbs.

Blacks would be able to own houses in areas such as Belvedere,

Mabelreign, Highlands, Greendale, Marlborough, Newlands, among others. Blacks would drive the posh cars driven by whites.

Blacks would be able to send their children to schools, which were a preserve for whites. Institutions like Umtali Boys High School, Umtali Girls High School, Umtali Junior School, Chancellor Primary School, Prince Edward, Queen Elizabeth, Lord Malvern, Peter House, Lomagundi, Victoria High School, Churchill, Gilford High School, John Cowie Primary to mention, but a few.

Once the tables were turned, whites would send their children to our community schools like Sakubva Secondary School, Dangamvura High School, Elise Gledhill, Mabvuku High School, Vhengere High School, Mucheke High Schools, Mzilikazi High School, George Stark, St Peters Kubatana, Kambuzuma High School, Gillingham High School, Amaveni High School, we were told during those *pungwe* rallies. We would be drilled into the essence of Chimurenga. There, we would be taught some slogans like, '*Icho charira kupiko? KuZimbabwe.*' Other slogans that we were taught were, '*Pamberi mberi nehondo, pasi nevadzvanyiriri, pasi navo, pasi nevatengesi, pasi navo, pasi nevasvetasimba.*'

CHAPTER 3

INFERIORITY COMPLEX

When hunger came gnawing into my tummy, Amai fished out a lunch box that she had stashed away in her small bag. When I opened the lunch box, an enticing aroma wafted into the coach.

Rice that had taken on a yellow colour from Madras curry powder and the roadrunner chicken roasted into a golden colour filled the coach.

I hungrily wolfed away on the appetising food ignoring a dozen or so of furtive and childish glances being cast in my direction by my age mates. Some of them would pluck up enough courage to ask for a few noodles of rice and others would resort to aping my eating habits and movements with awe.

Having exhausted the food, we would turn to games that would while up time. Games that would keep us awake whilst enjoying our cruise aboard the brown coaches.

I would fish out an old dog-eared gloss magazine passed on from Baba's white employer Baas Van de Merwe. We would divide the magazine into two.

We would claim whatever appeared on our side. We would say, '*Kwangu uku, mukadzi wangu, imba yangu, imbwa yangu, mota yangu, caravan yangu, sabhabha yangu.*' We all believed, brainwashed into believing that anything white was superior and next to Godliness.

Whites were incomparable then. You would hear the communities saying, '*Haikona kutamba nemwana wamisisi mhani akaoma.*'

Even during *sarura wako*, a pick and choose game of partners we would say, '*Wangu mutsvuku ane ndoro chena.*' Nobody would pick on a black partner ahead of a light-skinned one. It was all about the fairness of the skin than anything else that mattered most.

The lighter the skin, the fairer the person. The belief that the lighter the skin, the fortunate the person, still runs deep among Africans.

No wonder why those *black wadadas* or *black mambas* that we grew up with have resorted to applying some skin lightening creams or worse still consuming some skin lightening tablets.

Maybe there is an urgent need to decolonise the African mind or worse still exorcise the colonial demon whose tentacles have spread across the African mind.

Around 12 midnight, our eyes would be heavy with sleep having roamed and peeped through the length and breadth of the forests where we childishly believed that the horned devil prowled those grotesque forests nocturnally. Our mothers would prepare us for our retirement to bed under those wooden benches. They would sleep on the benches. Most of us then would not have graduated from bed wetting habits. To scare us, our mothers would threaten to unleash frogs into our pants.

Underpants then were fashioned like vests, those that had some air vents for ventilation. We would not wear underwear. Boys would go through primary education without having worn underwear. Underwear and shoes were a privilege.

Only black kids who hailed from working middle class families like black teachers, nurses, soldiers and police officers could afford to spoil their offspring with luxuries such as underwear and shoes.

The majority of us would only see those images in gloss magazines. To most of us, we never viewed that as lack because we were not used to that. We thought and childishly believed that underwear was a preserve for whites. We had never seen our fathers sporting them. After all, only white models appeared in those gloss magazines. In the morning, we would wake up at dawn. Our mothers would shepherd us to lavatories where we would be spruced up in readiness for the new day.

Our mothers would also go to great lengths to make their appearances acceptable in a city of Salisbury's status. Around 6am, the giant millipede would announce its arrival with a long and deafening honk of *kweeeeeee!*

A few minutes later, the train would saunter to an expected halt into the railway station. Salisbury reminded me of a story that Baba loved to narrate to us as we waited for supper in our *dare*, which was meant for males only. At the *dare* or *chivara*, male children were initiated into manhood. I remember Baba advising my elder brothers not to rush into marriages before owning a suit, an Oris wristwatch, a bed, a wardrobe and a bicycle.

He always reasoned that it would be impossible to purchase those things once one had plunged into marriage without them. A suit, a bicycle and a wristwatch were status symbols.

I recall one night Baba telling us how white Rhodesians became intimidated when one of them allegedly stumbled on a note that was allegedly authored by German dictator Adolf Hitler during the Second War.

Hitler had hinted in the alleged letter that he would be coming to have his lunch at Jameson Hotel, then one of Salisbury's elite hotels. Baba had said, when white Rhodesians got wind of the contents of the alleged missive, they abandoned their homes in Salisbury and drove out of the capital. That was how fearsome Hitler was. The mere mention of his name could see some white Rhodesians soiling their pants. And these were whites who perceived themselves to be superior to us, the rightful owners of the land.

These whites treated us as third class citizens. These were whites who treated us like trash, like some door rugs, like baboons, worse off than dogs, which they regarded as their best friends.

That missive alleged to have been attributed to Hitler exposed white Rhodesians who loved their *Super Rhodesia* with a passion.

Maybe they were also afraid of us deep down that was why they chose to segregate against us. They used divide and rule tactics to divide blacks. Whites, who were not racially allowed to mix and mingle with blacks, would use a flight of metal steps that hovered over the Harare station, steps that almost resembled the Birchenough Bridge structures.

They would always use ways and roads, which had signs *Europeans Only*. After going through the flight of stairs, they would be whisked away by taxis or their personal cars. And those who would be travelling to other cities and towns would board the Blue Arrow buses, buses that used star-studded hotels as their pick-up and drop points. It later dawned on me that not all white Rhodesians were racists.

Amai heaved her suitcase on her plaited and covered head, got hold of me by hand and towed me through a sea of fellow blacks, some of who looked lost in a big city like Salisbury.

As we crossed one of Salisbury's streets, which I cannot recall, Amai lost her footing sending me and the suitcase tumbling on the tarmac. A sleek Citroen vehicle, which we referred to as *datya* or *dafi*, missed us by inches.

The driver, a white bearded chap brought his hydraulic powered machine to a screeching halt. He heaved himself out of the vehicle and came charging at Amai swearing through pursed lips.

'*Sori Ngosi, pirizi Baas, ndiregerereiwo pirizi ndapota kani,*' Amai apologised. She picked up what had remained of her mangled *bhokisi*, stuffed back some clothes that were protruding for freedom. She panted, dusted herself and me before sitting a few yards from the pavement to regain her composure. Having regained composure, we resumed with our journey to Market Square where we boarded a Unifreight bus, bound for Gillingham. Each city then had a distinctive colour of buses that plied her routes. Salisbury had a maroon colour at the middle that blended well with a predominantly cream colour whilst Umtali had a blue colour that blended well with an off-white colour.

Bus crews then would also wear uniforms that matched those colours. They looked smart in those uniforms that were complimented with some berets. Those days *kwachu-kwachu* was unheard of. Vandalism was a criminal offence that attracted a hefty and deterrent fine or even a custodial sentence. No one dared to vandalise state property. Blacks feared the wrath of the law. Blacks feared police brutality.

Blacks feared for the worst should they dabble in such activities. Blacks feared to be charged with sabotage. Blacks feared to be arraigned before the courts, before hostile white judges. Before racially drugged public prosecutors. Before frowning clerks of courts, *vanamabharani.*

CHAPTER 4

COLONIAL BONDAGE

A system that was designed to stifle dissenting voices. A system that was perfected to prolong and perpetuate colonial rule. That was then and this is now.

Buses then did not display route markings just above the dashboard. Routes would be displayed in rolling bold letters at the top *Gillingham, Mufakose, Tafara, Kuwadzana, Mabvuku, Mbare, Sakubva, Dangamvura, Zimunya, Magwegwe, Lobengula, Mzilikazi, Mpopoma, Mutapa, Senga, Amaveni, Mkoba, Mucheke* to mention, but a few.

We finally boarded the bus to Gillingham. It was packed to the brim. Commuters, who were unfortunate to find unoccupied seats, sweated it out in the gangway, which they clutched to as if their lives depended solely on it.

When we arrived in Gillingham, we were given a hearty, rousing and warm reception. We were too many of us, crammed in a house too small to accommodate all of us.

We the young ones would sleep under a raised bed on which Amai and Amainini Jekunareta, her younger sister, would share since Babamunini Gorobheki was a night watchman at a local company. Whenever Babamunini Gorobheki returned home in the morning, he would try as much as he could to entertain his Amaiguru thereby depriving himself of quality sleep.

As much as he tried to be brave, he would finally succumb to sleep in a sitting posture mumbling words, which were both incoherent and inaudible.

Word went around then that Babamunini Gorobheki had been fed with heavy dosages of stay, soft, *mupfuhwira, kholobela*. His relatives believed *mupfuhwira* was the reason why he would always fall asleep in the middle of a conversation. Maybe he was, maybe not.

Three days later, we were on the move. We did not want to overstay our welcome. We visited Sekuru Kamiyosi who stayed in *Bharabhadhiya*,

Belvedere where he had secured employment as a cook. We were later informed that his employers were against Sekuru Kamiyosi housing his family in his servant's quarters.

That was the reason why most blacks who were employed in the Eastern suburbs were forced to keep their wives at their rural areas who they would visit annually as if they were a thirteenth cheque. I now know the reason why women then were able to bear children by the gross and yearly, *gore mwana, gore mwana*.

Bearing children by the gross then was something that was envied. Blacks then believed that any family that would have borne children by the gross would not feel much pain whenever God decided to take human tax. The mortality rate then was just too high. Infants could succumb to fontanel. I remember Amai lecturing young mothers about the effects of *nhova* and how it was treated.

Nhova came in different types and sizes. There was *ndongorongo*, which Amai said could be identified by some green like veins and spots that ran across the navel area.

Mothers then would bath their children with medicinal concoctions to cure *ndongorongo*. Some infants would be adorned with buttons tied to a tree bark, *rwodzi* or *bote* that would have been twisted into a string.

That bark would have been yanked from a tree with medicinal properties. You would think those infants would be wearing small watches. It wasn't swaggerish then to do so. Infants then would be bathed in water in which shells from oceanic snails would be snailing and whirling.

There was the type that was difficult to treat known in the medicinal parlance as *chipande*. That one if not treated could result in the head failing to hold at the centre. It would simply give in at the centre.

The elders then would say, 'Nhova yadhirikira.' It would take quite a beating to spruce the *chipande* up known then as *Kukwidza nhova inenge yave kutambira mukati*.

Apart from *nhova*, some children would have some difficulties in making some phonic sounds. Elders believed those children would have been tongue-tied by *rurembo*, which would be disentangled by the slice of a razor sharp razor blade. Then infants would be bathed in big homemade metal dishes known in the community parlance as *mabhavhu*. These were usually crafted by members of the original Johane Masowe sect founded by Shonhiwa *Susupenzi* Masedze of Gandanzara.

There were some children who possessed big navels, *makuvhu matende*, which could result in their shirts or blouses protruding out of their shorts or skirts. Shorts, shirts, dresses or blouses were multi-coloured as they were sewn or pieced together from cuts from the textile industries. The multi-coloured cloths were known in the ghetto parlance as *marabhi*.

These could be used as patches on torn clothes – *zvigamba*. Marabhis could also be used to sew some pillowcases, bed covers, *makhavhabhedhi* and aprons, which were worn by *mbuya dzemisika*.

As I grew up, I was taught in the ghetto to deliver a hard and low kick aimed at that protruding navel during street fighting.

It would weaken the victim. That priceless knowledge was imparted on me by martial arts students who would have been to various kung-Fu clubs dotted across Sakubva like Sango led by the late legendary Master Mushoriwa Zambuko, Lees Kung-Fu Club or Speed and Timing.

We watched some war movies in which we would hate some snipers and main actors who would destroy their enemies with a passion.

We would feel the pain as bullets riddled through bodies of enemies. We would clutch positions on which those enemies would have been shot. Blood would flow and meander like rivulets. The enemies would coil, groan, writhe, grimace and contort their faces in excruciating pain before passing on. Warplanes would bomb enemy territory razing high-rise buildings reducing them to debris.

Many casualties would be recorded during those air strikes. Victims especially women and children who would have been caught in crossfire as collateral damage, would wail for departed family members.

We would also wail for some of our relatives who were being caught in similar situations. Then the war that brought our hard fought independence was still raging and blazing on like a veld fire.

Our brothers and sisters were being bombed at Nyadzonia, Chimoio and Tembwe by the Rhodesian Front forces. We were losing our brothers and sisters in combats across the country and beyond our borders. The Rhodesian Front forces were also losing some of their battle hardened and fine service members, but would always choose to report using euphemism.

Their service members would always die in action. The number of their casualties would always be smaller as compared to those of the liberation fighters.

For that, we would hate them to the footprint. As a result, we detested war films because we sometimes felt wars were never meant to be won by those who would have been fighting for what was rightfully theirs – a worthy cause, the land, freedom and independence.

Whenever the film ended, the sign *THE END* would signal our exit from the hall.

CHAPTER 5

NOCTURNAL BREAD

It was natural and logical that intimacy that comes after a year of absence would surely be enjoyable and productive.

That applied to fields. Any field left fallow for a year under shift cultivation, would obviously be productive when ploughed. That field would give the farmer a ten-fold harvest. Remember also that then, conventional family planning methods were a preserve for whites.

Condoms then known as durex were again a preserve for whites. Blacks would use the withdrawal method, used natural means like calculating their fertile period.

Tradition had it then that it was difficult to impregnate a breast-feeding woman. That method was not efficient, no wonder why most children then fell sick or even died after having been lactated with contaminated breast milk known as *kuyamwisira*.

Most used some traditional herbs woven into a bark and tied at the waist. The husbands would simply snap that woven waist ring which in most cases blended well with waist beads.

Waist beads, which were adorned by women then together with middle finger long labia were viewed as husbands' play stations, old men's toys during foreplay. Some would go to great length of having some lacerations on their thighs.

Some traditional medicines that had the effect of arousing men's sexual desires would have applied on these lacerations, which were then known as *mastarters*. Then it was taboo for married women to shave off their pubic without the knowledge of their husbands.

Tradition demanded that only husbands had the right to shave off their wives' pubic hair. Any wife who would have shaved off their pubic hair without the blessings of their husbands would result in her being sent packing with a divorce token, *gupuro* which usually was in the form of a ten or five cent coin.

The shaving off pubic hair by a woman would be misconstrued as a sign of unfaithfulness. That was then and this is now.

Then the community would go to great length for the sake of sexual gratification of men. Women were brought up in communities that took pride in the schooling of women in bedroom antics like *Chinamwari*. Bed hopping by men would always be blamed on women who would have failed to satisfy their men in bed or worse still would have not been trained in the tenets of the bedroom call.

Sekuru Kamiyosi had devised a plan to hoodwink his employers who hated his family with a passion yet pretended to love him to bits.

He would shepherd us out of the yard at the crack of dawn, smuggle us after his employers would have gone off to work and expel us again before mid-morning as his bosses would return home for tea. We would stay in the servants' quarters before lunch to avoid being detected when the Harrisons returned for lunch.

We would return under the cover of darkness so that Ambuya Anzikariya would prepare supper for us. Sekuru Kamiyosi would make sure, he would have smuggled enough relish for supper.

Sekuru Kamiyosi would not allow us to play outside fearing we might be detected despite the *bhoyisikayi* being hedged off by the sprouting hibiscus barricade, which Ambuya Anzikariya sometimes would pluck for relish.

Even Ambuya Anzikariya's youngest child Pesonariti who was only two and still suckling, would not cry even when nature demanded so. She seemed to have been schooled to adhere to the world of silence.

A world of fear. A world of secrecy. A world in which blacks were inferior and as such expected to be loyal and submissive without questioning the status quo.

Little or young as she was, she knew she held the keys to the family's livelihood, Sekuru Kamiyosi's job. *But was that a job or pastime?*

Sekuru Kamiyosi insisted it was a job, a job that gave him some bragging rights over his unemployed contemporaries in Dande's Kamutsenzere village. It was a job that enabled him to smuggle for us some dog biscuits, which we would masticate hungrily. He insisted it was a job because it would give him a break from dried and ground okra, ground cowpeas and all relishes synonymous with the Dande area.

It was a job because it enabled him to benefit immensely from second hand clothes passed on by the Harrisons, glossy magazines, protection from the then marauding white police officers who would demand passes for one to be in the cities.

The job enabled him to enjoy European delicacies only found in hotels like Meikles and Jameson. The job enabled him free television rights, access to ice cold water, free electricity, occasional free booze, free newspapers journalised to the brim with propaganda, free news over the radio as well as some occasional parties, which were thrown by the Harrisons.

It was over the Harrisons' radio that he had heard his favourite song *Sevenza Josaya* then. He would sing it to us albeit in a low tone so as not to arouse the suspicion of the Harrisons.

After three days of playing hide and seek with the Harrisons, Amai decided it was time to return to Umtali by rail. We boarded the brown train back home to Umtali that night in 1975.

As the train glided, wriggled and wiggled her way out of the station in Salisbury, Amai and I could be seen waving hands to Sekuru Kamiyosi, Ambuya Anzikariya and family who marvelled at the train as it gathered momentum. They waved at us until a gloomy cloud of darkness enveloped them.

We kept waving until the train stopped at Mabvuku to pick up some passengers. I still wondered whether those waves by Sekuru Kamiyosi and Ambuya Anzikariya were genuine or were a sign of relief that we had finally left.

Sekuru Kamiyosi might have been relieved to know that he was finally going to enjoy the conjugal rights that he had missed during our stint at his one roomed *bhoyisikayi*.

The fact that he needed to enjoy his conjugal rights regularly was the sole reason why he had smuggled his wife into Salisbury.

In 1982, just two years after independence, I was back on the train to Harare. Zimbabwe had attained *uhuru* after a protracted liberation struggle that had been ignited by the 1966 *Chinhoyi Battle*.

A battle that had claimed the lives of seven gallant fighters of the *Second Chimurenga*, the likes of Chatambudza and Guzuzu.

In 1980, we had welcomed guerrillas into a plethora of assembly points. In Dangamvura, we had sung in unison and hilariously as ZANU PF campaigned in our hood.

'*Hona Mukoma Nhongo bereka sabhu tiende chauya chauya, hona Mukoma Nhongo bereka sabhu tiende pasi nedzakutsaku.*'

Following the announcement of election results that ushered

ZANU PF into power, the government organised an all-night independence gig, pungwe where the late Robert Nester Marley belted before a capacity crowd at Rufaro Stadium.

Zimbabweans from all walks of lives were bused and railed from other towns and cities to Harare to celebrate Zimbabwe's independence. There Cde *Chinx* sang, '*You better take the message to the Queen…Prince Charlie.*' The message that Prince Charles was supposed to convey to Queen Elizabeth was loud and clear. It was a message loaded with overtones of love, peace, reconciliation, harmony and above all the dawn of a new era, the independence of Zimbabwe.

Prince Charles had been handed over the remnants of the colonial regime, the *Union Jack* flag that was first hoisted on this land on September 12, 1890.

So strong was the euphoria of independence then, as we would sing some morale boosting songs.

CHAPTER 6

THE INDEPENDENCE EUPHORIA

The independence euphoria was very strong, in fact so strong that it could be touched and be felt.

We would sing *Nzira Dzemasoja* adapted from celebrated philosopher Mao Zedong of the Chinese Revolution fame.

A lot had changed on the coaches. There were no longer wooden benches. Instead, there were some hard seats made of plaster like shiny material, seats that were devoid of comfort.

We could afford to travel first class or better still just to have a glance of what the classes looked like, the beds, the linen and the lavatories.

The colour had been changed from brown and cream to blue, red and white, those were the colours of the freedom train, *chitima cherusununguko*. Zimbabweans would flock to various railway stations.

Rail remained the most sought after and cheapest mode of transport. As we jostled to embark onto the train, I still had vivid memories of my first journey by train.

Once inside we struggled to find seats. When we finally found them, the five of us, that is my two elder brothers, two sisters and I, we could hear music blaring loud and clear. Not to be outdone our elder brother, Bhudhi Masango who owned a suitcase or briefcase like Supersonic radio also started to play music on his radio. Songs like Jonah Moyo's *Chimutorai,* Thomas Mapfumo's *Joice, Zimbabwe* by Oliver Mtukudzi, Marshall Munhumumwe's *Makorokoto* entertained passengers.

The coaches would reverberate with the sounds of Mukanya's lyrics, the Sunrise Kwela Kings and the Harare Mambos weighed in. Indeed, a new dawn, a new dispensation had dawned in Zimbabwe.

Passengers would troop into coaches with good music. Kariba, Powercell or Eveready PL 9 and 10 batteries, powered radios then.

It was the Eveready PL 10, which was dark blue in colour that would last the longest than the other brands. We would nightly crawl in all coaches in search of good music and joy. Passengers would dance, gyrate, wiggle, wriggle and serenade to music of that time. Zimbabweans then would enjoy themselves as if there was no tomorrow.

Women of loose character would wriggle their bottoms seductively to sway men to them. Passengers would dance to Simon and Naison Mwakalili's gems, John Chibadura's *Mukoma Edmore, Kumusha Kwaambuya, Madiro*, Mighty Victoria C' Kings' *Liza Oloo, Selina, Rozalina Soda* and *Simone Agira*.

And music that had a Second Chimurenga influence like Harare Mambos' *Jongwe*, Flavian Nyati's *Nyadzonia* and Jonah Moyo's *Baba* kept the independence exhilaration afloat. *Huyai tibatane* by Chadoka and Chirwa, a reggae flavoured song was also a favourite with passengers.

We would sing along to songs by Brian Rusike of the Pied Pipers, songs like *We Go Say, we are the champions, we are the lions, Ruva Rangu and Reggae Sounds of Africa* from Jamaica.

Rusike had taken over the mantle from the equally gifted Gideon Neganje who had kept the spirit of Chimurenga alive with some hard-hitting gems.

When the train arrived at Odzi, vendors flooded windows on both sides of the coaches. Vendors with all sorts of wares would besiege the train at Nyazura, Rusape, Eagles' Nest, Macheke, Marabada, Marondera, Mabvuku and Harare.

When we finally arrived in Harare, we used that flight of stairs to go over the train, stairs that were originally reserved for whites.

As the majority of Zimbabweans started to travel by train, whites stopped riding on the freedom train. Maybe to them freedom was an insult. They had stopped cruising on the train not because standards had plummeted, if anything standards were improving in leaps and bounds.

By then the government had electrified the railway line that linked Harare and Bulawayo up to Dabuka. An electric train plied the Harare-Bulawayo route up to Dabuka.

What an achievement by the new black government. Zimbabweans who would refer to anyone learned as *Mutumbuka*, after Dzingai Mutumbuka the first Education Minister.

Load shedding was unheard of, electricity was always available, omnipresent and ever present. After alighting from the train, we boarded an Emergency Taxi, ET, which came in the form of Peugeots 404 and 504 station wagons.

From Mbare Musika we went to Matapi Flats' Block 7's C floor where a sister of ours lived.

CHAPTER 7

PERILOUSLY PERCHED

I joined some ghetto youths who were perilously perched on the balcony overlooking Matapi Bar. As we sat perched there, we had a bird's eye view of the waterhole. I would marvel at scenes from the bar.

There some revellers would gyrate to music from the jukebox. As I was held spellbound by some dancing queens of the night, I was grabbed from behind by my sister, the one who resided in Mbare.

She gave me a thorough hiding. The only crime that I had committed was that of having perched dangerously as if I were a daredevil.

I had thrown caution to the wind in my childish stupor. I had forgotten the saying that says, 'a coward dies nine times before the actual death.'

After recovering from pangs of the beatings, I decided to visit the toilet as nature had been calling me for long. So smart were the toilets that one could then be forgotten for having mistaken the toilets for a kitchen.

The toilets smelled nice, were full of aroma, no taps leaked then. Electricity gave the interior an appealing look during the night. The paint on the block of flats then never shed tears of redress. The flats then, which used to house bachelors before independence, were in an imposing state. Then the flats could rival those in the Avenues area.

Most occupants of Matapi Flats were plucked from some nearby farms like Raffin, Mupunzani and some illegal settlements where Nyau dancers were abound.

Legend had it then that Nyau dancers had the power to take foetus from pregnant mothers, which they would take to graves where they would change into their frightening regalia.

Allegations were that once they were through with their dancing competitions, they would return the foetuses into their mothers' wombs.

Pregnant women were thus warned to stay away from Nyau dancers. Legend also had it that there were times when Nyau dancers would force members of the communities in which they stayed, into joining their dancing clubs.

The dancers, who would engage in festivities known as *kamwimwi,* would run after anyone who they would have picked on for initiation.

Once you tumble down in the process, picked up an injury, picked yourself up and manage to make good your escape from the clutches of Nyau dancers, that wound would never heal until you asked for forgiveness from them.

Legend also had it that Nyau dancers would not take it lightly to anyone who would stray to their changing houses, usually graveyards.

The environs of Mbare then were spick and span. Hostels like Matererini, Tagarika, and Chishawasha were worth living in. Rentals would regularly be paid at the local municipal offices known then as *kwakatsekera.* The *katsekeras,* council offices and beer gardens a deliberate departure from *mabhawa,* were manned by municipal police officers, known as *mawhite cap* in Harare.

In Mutare, municipal police officers were referred to as *magumbojena* because they always wore some white protectors or leg guards that would protect them against snakebites.

The town police officers or *mabhurakwachas* used to put on some shiny brown leg protectors that always left us dazzled and mesmerized with their shiny appeal. We always envied them. We would die to enlist in the police force just to have a feel of those leg protectors.

Then there were those who were referred to as police reserve, those who maintained peace and tranquillity in the tribal trust lands.

CHAPTER 8

WHAT'S IN A NAME?

Most beer gardens bear queer names like Mapitikoti, Rambanai, Chidzere, Chikomo, Mushando, Manhede to mention, but a few.

Manhede in Mucheke, Masvingo and Rambanai at Jerera Growth Point really got me thinking. Why would councillors or City Fathers and Mothers in all their wisdom get to name a waterhole Mapitikoti, Manhede or Rambanai?

Mapitikoti maybe because beer goes down better with women. The wisemen from the Eastern Highlands of Manicaland, *wane Samanyika* have an age-old traditional saying that goes, *'Mhamba ingonaka nawamai.'*

Rambanai was issued as a warning to couples who were in the habit of going for beer drinking binges together that they risked going separate ways. *Why?* Many activities took place in beer gardens, bars and nightclubs.

So intoxicating was the local brew in Masvingo that when consumed to excess would surely knock imbibers off balance, leaving them lying with legs astride, arms folded at the back of the head whilst staring into the blank sky. Such was the potency of the brew. Each city then had her own brand of opaque beer. Mutare had *Kariba Mhamba* and later *Pungwe*, Harare had *Rufaro*, which was brewed, marketed and distributed by Rufaro Marketing, Bulawayo had *Ingwebu* and *Indlovu* whilst Gweru had *Super* and *GoBeer*.

Those were the days of *Takura 5* and *Takura 10* opaque beer packaged in a plastic pack that was housed in a khakhi cardboard box container shaped in the mould of a shake-shake.

Some joy seekers or night crawlers would be carried away by cheap bar talk. Some beer guzzlers would be fooled by infatuate love from some thigh vendors.

Some lovers of wisdom waters would pretend to be wiser and start jabbering in the Queen's language, a language they would never attempt to speak in their sober states.

Some philanthropists who would have bought them beer until they dropped drunk, until they staggered home or worse get wheel-barrowed home with soiled pants would carry some married women away.

Some marriages were left tottering on the brink of collapse after some revellers would have fondled some tired boobs and bums of married women in the presence of their husbands, husbands who would have pretended to have had one too many.

Some married women were left counting the costs of frequenting watering holes after some secret admirers whose proposals they would have turned down sexually ravaged them. After those sexual assaults, the secret admirers in their drunken stupors would brag about that to their drinking partners who would turn them in when relationships went sour. Some marriages were left on the rocks after married women would have engaged in strip shows after having drowned in a sea of beer.

Some marriages were left hanging by threads after some married women who would have behaved like loose cannons, would have dressed down their husbands with unprintable words in the full glare of fellow patrons.

Some marriages were left beyond redemption after some married women would have drawn lines of comparisons in as far as manhood and bedroom performances of their husbands and that of numerous men they would have bedded behind the backs of their husbands.

A lot of shenanigans were schemed, phrased, composed, packaged and implemented from these places.

CHAPTER 9

TEARS OF BRUTALITY

The aroma of oranges filled the bus in which passengers were packed like sugar beans. The bus that was heavy with the *Korekore* accent would occasionally stop to drop off passengers along the way.

Some passengers would occasionally stop to listen to our conversations, which were laced with a heavy *Manyika* accent.

Others would laugh at us, likening our adopted language to *Sena*, a Mozambican dialect. In our borrowed *Manyika* accent, we would also not understand what they would be saying.

Fits of laughter would confirm that these passengers would have shared some jokes. All we could hear of the language was nothing, but the movement and twitching of lips.

To us, it seemed like they were speaking double Dutch. We believed they were speaking another of those many Mozambican dialects, like *Sena*.

Surely having lived in Mutare where Mozambicans roamed surrounding villages, far longer than we had stayed in Dande, we should have been forgiven for detecting some similarities between the languages.

I realised then that all languages were important and as such had to be accorded respect. Any new language earned and learned added value to the person who would have acquired it. Renowned multi-linguists of this world started with their mother languages before adding foreign languages to their linguistic belts.

I realised that everyone was a foreigner, somehow, somewhere and anyhow. We were foreigners in Mutare where we were derogatorily referred to as *mabvakure*.

We were foreigners in both worlds. That is both in our adopted home and in the land on which our umbilical cords were tied and buried under the ground to create a long lasting bond with our ancestors.

When we finally arrived at *Dande Storo*, we had been exhausted having travelled through a bumpy road that stretched through to Mukumbura border post. Mukumbura remains the official gateway to Mozambique.

We trudged through dusty pathways or labyrinths that criss-crossed Chipiso village, under heavy loads of groceries. We went straight to our paternal grandmother Ambuya Marujata who was glad to see us after years of living far from home among foreigners.

Foreigners who spoke a foreign language. Foreigners whose norms and values we were still struggling to come to grips with. Norms, values and survival skills of aliens whose ropes we were still labouring to grasp.

After exchanging some pleasantries with Ambuya Marujata, she broke into a wail, wailing for relatives who had perished during the Second Chimurenga.

She had also shed a tear or two over the then colonial establishment's brutality and the pain of neglect that she had suffered at the hands of her surviving children. As tradition dictated, we joined her in wailing for relatives that had passed on during our absence.

Relatives whose images our photographic memories had deleted from our memory banks. After comforting each other and wiping off tears that had trickled and cascaded down our cheeks, Ambuya Marujata sent for a good number of our relatives who did not have wind of our arrival. A cavalcade of humanity led by our Tetes among them Muchadura, Mandiramba, Nhamoyembereko, including Nhamoyerombe, Nhamoyebonde, Mushayabvudzi and Hunidzashe trooped into the dilapidated compound that was weeping and praying for salvation, for a miracle, for a resuscitation, for a revival.

The grass thatching on Ambuya Marujata's living room known in the village parlance as *dhanduru* had not only gone off colour due to the vagaries of a barrage of harsh weather conditions, but the roof was slowly curving in under the weight of some makeshift roofing trusses.

So porous was the roof that we could gaze at stars whilst sleeping under. Sleeping in that hut was tantamount to sleeping in the open. We simply did not have a roof over our heads. Our heads were roofless. The other hut that Ambuya Marujata referred to as her kitchen was worse off. A camouflage of soot dangled perilously over our heads. So low was the roof that we had to bend over whenever we were negotiating our way in. So leaky was the roof that it did not have the capacity to starve off even some drizzles.

CHAPTER 10

TEARS OF NEGLECT

The huts were simply neglected and desperately needed to be spruced up to give them a homely face. Ambuya Marujata later revealed to us that the huts had deteriorated to ramshackle status during the war of liberation when villagers were rounded and moved into a protected village at Pachanza known then in the Chimurenga phraseology as *mukeep*.

After exchanging some traditional greetings, our Tetes and Babamukuru Mairosi demanded that we got our hairs shaved off to show grief and respect for the departed. We felt sorry for Bhudhi Masango who had been caring for his afro hair for nearly a decade.

He had refused to have that hair shaved off or trimmed even though it constantly got him into trouble with the Rhodesian Front soldiers who always suspected him of being a *gandanga*.

Those tasked with the tradition were not skilled barber persons. All they were required to do was to remove the hair from the head. They were not interested in the appearance of the person who would have gone through their ordeal. In most cases, the pairs of scissors would not have been sharp and efficient as demanded by such tasks. In desperate attempts to sharpen them, our elders would use firewood charcoal as makeshift files. Because of the bluntness of those pairs of scissors that could be used to shave off hairs of almost the entire village, the hair shaves would not be even. Those days, only a few would visit barbershops like Meikles to have their hair trimmed or cut.

We had to mourn for the loss of Bhudhi Masango's pride, his hair. We had to shed tears, not crocodile ones, but genuine and irritating tears for Bhudhi Masango's hair, hair that over the years had become his trademark.

Hair that had endeared him so well with the fairer sex whose hearts he used to break on the spur of a moment.

I doubt if those girls did have hearts for real because the frequency those so called hearts were captured, broken into smithereens, closed for temporary renovations and re-swung, opened their doors to Bhudhi Masango after some sweet talking, defied logic.

'Where do broken hearts go?' One singer had once asked in the 80s. But then this subject they called love was difficult to comprehend. A lot of people tended to swim with the tide of love when they get drugged or rather intoxicated with the loveholic effects.

Most of those who would have readmitted Mukoma Masango were left suckling kids whose paternity he would be quick to deny. Most of those babies I later gathered were conceived in the bush Bhudhi Masango was a bhundu boy. Products of his manhood or seeds remained, *vana vemusango*, kids born out of wedlock, bastards. These unpalatable, despicable habits of his, surprisingly endeared him with the fairer sex.

Most girls who would have been waiting for their turn to be devoured in the same bush by Bhudhi Masango who had turned it into his love nest and rendezvous, would quickly come to his defence should their rivals fell pregnant.

You would hear them saying, 'Ha *ivo machukazi acho akableya. Kuitiswa mimba musango shuwa? Dai ndiri ini ndakange ndisingabvumi.*'

Come their turn to be laid and wolfed, they too would succumb to the same modus operandi of Bhudhi Masango.

CHAPTER 11

LUCK CHARMS

I believed and still do that Bhudhi Masango must have been using those love concoctions prescribed by Sekuru Magwenzi-Mutombo whose prowess and expertise in the African medicine was astonishing, flabbergasting, astounding and just spellbinding.

Any man, who would have consulted him over *mushonga wemaraki,* would be left singing heaps of praises. No lady or girl would turn down a love proposal from anyone who would have sought Sekuru Magwenzi-Mutombo's assistance.

Job seekers would also queue up for his services. But then jobs were not as scarce as they are these days. Then job seekers could afford to hold white employers to ransom. White employers would go on bended knees pleading with competent and highly skilled employees not to walk out on them.

White employers then could afford to promise heaven, the moon and earth to their favourite employees. But then you would not just wake up to become a favourite employee in a company that had thousands of employees under its books.

That favour could only find your way only after you had visited Sekuru Magwenzi-Mutombo. Even those who worked for whites in the leafy or Eastern suburbs would troop to consult Sekuru Magwenzi-Mutombo for his endearment charms.

The charms would swiftly change the hearts of the employers. Employees who used those charms would always get the lion's share of attention, wages, ration perks, second hand clothing and wage advancement from white employers.

Those days, workers earned wages whose minimums and the government gazetted maximums. Workers could apply for a double wage or pay leave whenever they decided to go on leave. That means, come month end, they would not be paid for they would have been waged already.

That would put a strain on their finances, a strain that would see most of them plunging or rather playing into the hands of some loan sharks. Better still, employees would torment their employers for another advance. That was then and this is now.

We had to stay for a few days to grow our hairs to evenness. During those few days, Bhudhi Masango was thrice hauled before the village court.

He was being charged with defiling half a dozen girls whom he had charmed with his good looks, airs or bragging rights, charms supplied by Sekuru Magwenzi-Mutombo as well as a concoction of promises and lies.

He would brag about his employers, the Stephens in Darlington, Mutare. He would brag about how well waged he was back in Mutare. He would brag about his fleet of bicycles, the Perry, the Three Speed, Sports' Bike as well as the Hodha Bike; the one that had a large compartment at the front, a compartment in which a 50kg of mealie-meal could fit comfortably.

Most of those girls who were beautiful terribly lacked the mental aptitude to match the cunningness of Bhudhi Masango.

The girls, who were blinded by their status of being village belles, were not naïve, but foolish to have fallen for a ladies' man, a Lothario, a man who could sweet talk them into dropping their pants for him in the middle of the bhundu.

But then the girls naïve as they were, would report for other amorous sessions or encounters all in the hope of trying to win his heart.

Unfortunately, for those girls, Bhudhi Masango did not have a heart. He seemed to have traded his heart and soul to the devil. His actions were diabolical.

He had warmed the hearts of the village queens when they came to dance to the music from his radio. His radio was the only one in the village that never seemed to run out of power.

CHAPTER 12

PROMISES AND LIES

The girls would compete for his attention as they would wriggle, wiggle and shake their bums with reckless abandon. He would occasionally call those he would have lusted into our makeshift traditional boys' bedroom.

There he would feast on some of those girls. Their wails of pain and feigned resistance would be drowned by the blaring music. He would promise to take them along with him to Darlington. He would promise to pay the bride price for them. He would convince them to have their dowries ready for the migration to Mutare. He would promise to facilitate their fast track into marriage.

Bhudhi Masango had played his cards closer to his chest. He had managed to evade detection by parents and guardians of girls he had been abusing for the past few weeks.

He would buy the silence of some of the parents and guardians by making booze, the intoxicating *kachasu* brand.

The cat was finally let out of the bag. The deeds of his voracious manhood was finally exposed from his pants when two girls he had slept with, got entangled in a heated exchange of disparaging war of words that had taken place at Chivaravara River. During the tongue-lashing contest between the girls who behaved like some rabid canines resulting in a cat skirmish, Bhudhi Masango's name cropped up. That was how his name got dragged into the mud.

According to highly placed sources, all hell broke loose when a group of girls who were modelling on the riverbanks started to draw lines of comparisons among their God given bodily assets.

Things came to a point when the two lasses Hamundidi and Hamunyari unknowingly laid claim on Bhudhi Masango.

Hamundidi is said to have poked fun at Hamunyari by telling her off her face that even though she appeared to be as slim as a pencil line, she had managed to turn and spin the head of the newest and hottest man in the village, Bhudhi Masango. Unbeknown to Hamundidi that she was dating a multi-timing, she went on to brag about how good in bed or rather in the bhundu Bhudhi Masango was.

But Hamundidi should not have bragged about how well between the sheets Bhudhi Masango was. A bhundu boy, he was, a bhundu boy he would remain. Other girls who had been robbed of their pride of womanhood joined in the fray.

But these ones were not robbed of their pride, they seemed to have surrendered voluntarily and seemed to have been in a compliance of some sort or competition to lose their *chiremera*. The girls fought on village lines, as if they were fighting over the control of the river. Some head boys who were heading cattle nearby heard the hubbub and resolved to investigate what had thrown the once serene and tranquil village into turmoil.

Unprintable words were being launched at each other, flying thick and fast. When they drew closer, the boys were taken aback by what they had seen. Village girls were fighting over a ghetto boy whilst in the nude.

They quickly took to their heels and dashed for a nearby homestead where elders were enjoying their traditional seven days' brew.

The boys, who were heavily panting for breath, narrated all that they had witnessed at the river.

Elderly women, clad in their wrapping clothes and blouses that had seen better days to the point of showing their backs, staggered off to the river where a spectacle of nudity awaited them.

CHAPTER 13

ACT OF ABOMINATION

Nothing of that sort had happened in their lives. It was taboo and an abomination to them. They had agreed in their drunken and elderly stupor that such an incident heralded a bad omen.

When the elderly women, five of them drew closer to the river between, they stripped trees of their branches, which they intended to use to lash at the girls with.

The quintet was then breathing fire and brimstone. When the girls realised that they were under siege from the elderly women, they took to flight in that naked state bearing down the homestead where elders were drowning their sorrows.

Some took refugee into a nearby changing house, a makeshift bathroom made of grass, which is a multipurpose structure, used as a bathroom, urinary and changing room, synonymous with bad odours that pervaded the air every time a person visited it.

The elderly men who had last seen youthful nude girls during their youthful days, scrambled to feast their eyes on the free manifestation.

Some of them could be heard shouting in their drunken stupor, '*Mwari wakanaka nhasi adzora ndangariro mumaziso edu.*'

The group of shameless elderly men only scampered away from the *chinjausi* where the girls were then huddled together shying away from the prying and scanning elderly eyes. Eyes that were devoid of shame and dignity. The quintet handed the girls their clothes after a thorough hiding that left them wailing on top of their voices and pleading for mercy.

The following day, the village Head Taguma Tugamba-Tukawanda who had got wind of the girls' misdemeanours summoned them to his Village Court where he intended to get to the bottom of the issue.

When the trial of the girls who were being charged with indecent exposure that had put the good standing of their families and village into disrepute kicked off, the girls owned up and revealed what had really transpired.

That was when Bhudhi Masango's name was mentioned as having been in the eye of the storm. He was swiftly summoned to the Court where he was to answer similar charges with the girls, charges that had been classified as serious.

It was during the trial that six girls revealed that Bhudhi Masango who had promised to marry them in the not too distant future had deflowered them. Following the revelation, parents and guardians of the girls blew up their top accusing Bhudhi Masango of having ruined the futures of their daughters.

'*Ndiani acharima makura ako iwe Mwendamberi? Kana wanga wajaira kutambisa vana vevanhu kwaMutare ikoko manje wairasa. Isu hatina vana vanotambiswa tiri maKorekore. Hokoyo nezvivanda*,' they threatened.

Lest they had forgotten, we were also *Korekores* whose roots and navels were deep rooted and interred in that land too. Bhudhi Masango was slapped with a fine of seven goats, six as damage or compensation for deflowering the six girls and the seventh for cleansing the mayhem that had reigned supreme in the village.

The girls' show was traditionally believed to have had angered a spirit medium of the land, a *mhondoro* known as *Mukweverera*, a revered rainmaker. Bhudhi Masango who had pleaded guilty to the seven counts, tried in vain to appeal for a lesser charge arguing that he intended to marry the six girls.

He argued that there was nowhere he was going to raise the fines within three days given. As such, Bhudhi Masango appealed for more time to pay the fine.

Ambuya Marujata disowned Bhudhi Masango, arguing that there was no way, the Court was going to attach her goats as compensation for a crime committed by a grandchild whose father was yet to be briefed on the case. And besides, paying such a hefty penalty would leave her poorer and wallowing in abject poverty. She also argued that those goats, which the Court was eyeing, belonged to her late husband. The court after weighing submissions by Ambuya Marujata and Bhudhi Masango, allowed him time to pay.

CHAPTER 14

PEEPING TOM

But was it time to pay or to abscond? The Court should have known that Bhudhi Masango could be a flight risk. Before footprints of those who had congregated at Sabhuku Tugamba-Tukawanda's court could be swept away, it was my turn to be dragged at the same Court for crimen injuria.

On an unknown date, I had gone to the river between Chivaravara in the company of my sisters where we intended to do some laundry in preparation for our journey back to Harare.

After hanging out our clothes to dry, we started to swim and frolicking in the clear water. Teenage boys and girls including male and female siblings could swim and bath together without any evil intentions. Teenage boys and girls all in the nude could be seen enjoying themselves in the water, scrubbing each other's backs without harbouring any sinister motives.

We became sexually active well into our twenties. Even though tradition allowed us to bath together, it outlawed boys even those who were still to drift into their teens to share baths with their mothers or other women.

After bathing with fellow teenagers, I took leave, leaving clothes that I had dried with my sisters. I only took with me Ambuya Marujata's zambia after lying to my sisters that I intended to wrap myself to ward off the effects of a cold breeze that was beginning to blow through the river.

I had something sinister up my sleeve. I stealthily manoeuvred my way through thick Mopani bushes that formed part of the vegetation that overlooked Nyatande River where women used to bath.

Tradition demanded that whenever a villager approached a river that was known to have designated bathing points, that person was required to announce their arrival in case they were people of the opposite sex who could have been bathing.

I crawled to a vantage point that hid me from the eyes of women who would have been taking their baths. I swiftly spread Ambuya Marujata's zambia, to make myself comfortable and waited for my prey. The river appeared deserted, seemed to be in agreement with the environment.

Before making myself comfortable on Ambuya Marujata's zambia, I had sprinkled *uriri,* some powder that was sourced from some climbing plants that had the effect of making anyone who would have come into contact with it to scratch endlessly.

It left marks like those of *munyawiri* or *nganya.* *Nganyas* are Mopani-like worms that can make those who would have encountered them scratch like nobody's business.

Birds that usually sang melodies that serenaded and blended well with the flow of the water were singing their usual ballads, some ballads of contentment.

But that day seemed to be different from other days. They seemed to be singing some melodies of shame, melodies of exposure. The birds of the air appeared to have been working in cahoots with other unforeseen forces of nature to expose me.

A few minutes later, two youngest wives of Sabhuku Tugamba-Tukawanda appeared onto the scene. The two women were really beautiful. They both looked radiant, well cared for by Sabhuku Tugamba-Tukawanda, well attired and above all, well-crafted by their Maker.

Legend had it that Sabhuku Tugamba-Tukawanda got married to the duo after winning battles against a local teacher and nurse who were dying to lay claim on them.

The two women had just arrived from Harare where they had been staying when the village Head immediately announced his intention of adding them to his two other conquests. He only succeeded after parting with a fortune in the form of cattle, which was then used to measure a man's worth.

The two women were yet to bear children for Sabhuku Tugamba-Tukawanda. Legend had it that the village Head, fearing that those he had beaten to the hands of the jewels might try their luck, had fenced them with a central locking system, *rukaho rwebanga.*

Those privy to him claimed that *rukaho* was administered by a Mozambican *sangoma* from across Mukumbura border post. The duo took off their clothes before getting down to some serious bathing business. The environment savoured, drooled over and admired.

Two little naughty eyes preying and prying behind some thick bushes, were also savouring, drooling and admiring the naked queens, Queens of the Waters, Queens of the River, Queens of Nudity, Beauty Queens and the embodiment of beauty.

A pair of eyes that belonged to a Mutare stationed Peeping Tom who laid among the thick bushes of Dande, was roaming and surveying with enjoyment and contentment, assets of the village's most powerful political figure, the *Sabhuku*.

Those eyes were scanning the beauty of village belles on whom the kraal Kingpin had paid a fortune not only to lay claim on but also to view in their nude state. I did not mind about developing a boil like pimple on the lower eyelid then known as *shohwera*, which befell Peeping Toms and Peeping Theresas.

I occupied myself by marvelling at the beauty of the women's bodies as they took their time bathing and gambolling in the waters. Trouble started when they started to apply some Ponds.

A wasp stung me.

I sprang up, yelling, leaving behind Ambuya Marujata's wrapping cloth. Little did I know that I had blown up my cover. A team of nearby herd boys rushed to my aid. The kraal Head's wives were taken aback by the twist of events. They stood there, arms at akimbo, naked, radiant and glowingly beautiful. The herd boys had a field day in sampling the anatomy of the kraal Head's wives. When sense finally prevailed over them, they suddenly panicked, grabbed their clothes, which they had placed on *uriri* and hurriedly dressed up.

In no time, they were scratching as *uriri* sunk in. The women who had never tasted the effects of *uriri*, tried to rub off the powdery species with water.

CHAPTER 15

HOISTED BY MY OWN PETARD

Unbeknown to them, they were increasing the intensity of the rare *uriri*. The women cried aloud to their husband who happened to have been coming from *Dande Storo* where he had been drinking with the local leadership.

He swiftly came to the rescue of his wives. An overzealous and observant herdboy picked up Ambuya Marujata's wrapping cloth and went on to question about how it had come to be where it was.

Shaking with fearm and still to recover from the effects of wasp stings, I told him that I had spread it there as I intended to shoot some birds with my catapult.

Unfortunately, I could not produce the catapult neither could I produce some stones with which I should have been using to shoot down birds. Probed and prodded further, I owned up. I had dismally failed to build an excuse.

I told those present that I had been playing Peeping Tom at the two struggling women. I also revealed that I was responsible for sprinkling *uriri* at the bathing site. That did not go down well with Sabhuku Tugamba-Tukawanda who lashed at me sending me sprawling onto the ground.

He ordered me to remove all my clothes after which he instructed me to roll over. I complied with his diabolical and snarling orders, orders that could have made the devil green with envy.

Satisfied with the amount of *uriri* that had stuck to me like lynch, he sent me plunging into the river for a good measure. I was being hoisted by my own petard. I had been given to taste a concoction of my own bitter medicine.

I wept uncontrollably, weeping for my body that was burning with the effects of scratching. Satisfied with the punishment he had meted on me, he allowed me to dress up before force-marching me to our homestead, which was five stones' throw from Nyatande River.

Lathering at the mouth and with his two wives as evidence of my misdemeanours, he narrated the ordeal that I had put his wives through apart from having Peep Tomed on them.

'*Wabvisa madzimai vaSabhuku chiremerera chose. Unofanira kuripa pamwe nekurangwa zvakaomarara kuti uve chidzidzo kune dzimwe nhavatava dzakaita sewe. Ndopika ini mwana wemuera nzou yawapara iyi ihombe, ungasongorere madzimai asabhuku iwe?*' Ranted the kraal Head.

I was later dragged to the kraal Head's Court where I was to be tried for my transgressions. In no time, the village was awash with news of my shenanigans. The entire village trooped in droves to the kraal Head's Court where I was to appear before the emotionally charged kraal Head.

When villagers had gathered at the Court for the case to be heard, Ambuya Marujata and Babamukuru Raison objected to my trial by the kraal Head.

Their argument was that it was not proper in the eyes of natural justice for Sabhuku Tugamba-Tukawanda to preside over a case in which he was the complainant. He had to recuse himself if natural justice were to take place.

There was need for the case to be tried by a neutral Headman. He tried to object to the duo's argument, but his advisory team overruled his objection.

It was unanimously agreed that the case be referred to Sabhuku Maminimini who was also known as *Mutongi Gava*.

When the day of reckoning finally arrived, Sabhuku Maminimini's Court was teeming with balding and grey heads. After all submissions were made, we all waited in bated breath for the ruling.

I was let off the hook with a suspended sentence after Sabhuku Maminimini took into consideration the fact that Sabhuku Tugamba-Tukawanda had taken the law into his own hands by lashing at me before subjecting me to the harshness of *uriri*.

Sabhuku Tugamba-Tukawanda vowed to appeal against the ruling, which he said was flawed, and a blatant injustice.

Two days later, Ambuya Marujata sent us packing to Harare where we would connect to Mutare where we were treated as aliens. I had overheard her saying to her close ally and confidante Mbuya Rudhiya, '*Vana vemuchoni vachanditadzisa kugara zvakanaka muno mumusha.*' She had

had enough of us. She argued that we had strained her relationships with members of the community that treated us like aliens.

None of the two homes we had called homes were prepared to offer us sanctuary and comfort. Both viewed us with suspicion. Both were not prepared to take us in as one of their own. Both felt we belonged somewhere, somewhere, where exactly.

CHAPTER 16

CHRISTMAS EVE

I woke up with a start, the same start that you would have if you were to wake up in a mortuary under siege from an army of hallucinating corpses. Beads of sweat that had formed on my forehead started to cascade like a deluge, down my cherubic face.

I had just awoken from a nightmare that had left me energy sapped. I could see some streaks of moonlight streaming into our ramshackle church whose door was being besieged by a team of termites.

It indeed was under siege from the marauding red headed big termites. The door that cut a grotesque and sorry story of our church, perilously hung by a thread.

Eyes of all congregants that threatened to pop out of their sockets got glued to a dilapidated wall clock that chimed on the pole and dagga wall of the makeshift church.

As the dilapidated wall clock that dangled on the pole and dagga ramshackle church sauntered towards 12 midnight on the eve of Christmas Day in the mid70s, all the youths' eyes, which had become too heavy with sleep, suddenly popped out of their sockets in awe and anticipation. A hullabaloo erupted disturbing the serenity and tranquillity that had been reigning supreme in Fern Valley.

The suburb that is tucked away along the Mutare-Masvingo highway was a preserve for whites. Baba, *vaMuvhangeri* of the Premier Harvest Pentecostal Assembly led us in songs that heralded the birth of Christ. That day was just not any other day.

It was not an ordinary day, but a day endowed with a meaning to Christians across the globe. Christians from all lifestyles and even those under colonial bondage.

The day gave them an impetus to live and fight another day. It renewed their vigour to fight for their independence. It spurred them to fight against the oppressors of this world, those who were bend on stifling voices of reason.

Those who were out to extinguish the revolutionary inferno. Those who were out to pluck eyes from the sockets of visionaries. Those who were determined to throw spanners into the works of liberators.

Those who were out to derail the freedom train. All of a sudden, the church was plunged into song and dance. Suddenly all those who had retired to bed just outside the makeshift church, staggered into the church as if they were under the effects of an illicit brew. All of a sudden, the church hurtled and hurled into an oasis of activity. Young girls who would have just drifted into their teens and had been busy preparing tea for the congregants would troop into the church struggling with heavy potfuls of tea, *tea hobvu*.

All of a sudden, the church would be turned into a mini restaurant in which a mouth-watering aroma of fresh bread.

Bread for ordinary members of the church was served in winnowing bowls, *tsero*. Bread was dished out like confetti at a wedding.

Tea for ordinary members of the church was served from large teapots and their tea was not as heavy as that served to *Mufundisi* and his inner circle who would be sitting at a high table.

Tea for ordinary members had sugar stirred into it. Mufundisi and his cronies that included deacons, *madhikoni*, had the luxury of being served with super tea without sugar. They would extravagantly be doled out with basinful Gold Star white sugar to accompany or rather to sweeten their tea. That brand of white sugar was a preserve for whites for they were white and anything white was superior and deserved to be treated with some whitish respect.

Mufundisi and his blue-eyed boys would eat from breakable plates. Drank from breakable cups and drawn their tea from breakable teapots.

Apart from that, they also had the luxury of being lavishly pampered with homemade bread known then as *mafuturamvana*, fat cooks, cookies, *mafete* or some Choice Assorted biscuits.

I vividly recall how teenage girls then were swept away off their feet by the mere mentioning of the name. Quite a number of teenage girls had eloped to boys who could afford to spoil them with those biscuits. No wonder a sizeable number of children born out of those unions were christened Choice. Most of us envied, dreamt or rather aspired to be Mafundisi. Most ladies yearned to be *Mai Mufundisi*, pastors' wives. But back then congregants or rather people would not aspire or dreamt of becoming *Vafundisi*.

They would rather wait to be divinely called to the Holy House of the Lord by the Lord Himself and not by somebody else. They strived to walk the long, straight and narrow path as dictated by the Lord.

Vafundisi would not dabble in diabolic acts like bedding and impregnating scores of unattached single women, the divorced, widowed, those attached under the customary law and the legally married ones under the guise of deliverance.

Mafundisi would not stoop so low as to be involved in tomfooleries, unholy alliances and devilish acts. They were not referred to as *vanhu vaMwari* or Men of God.

Maybe they were not Godly then or maybe they were not as pious, morally upright, prayerful and prophetic as their modern day counterparts religiously and hegemoneously claim to be.

Moms would stay at home and dads would go and slug it out for the family. Brothers would enlist into the Army in defence of their pride, their nation, their motherland and sisters would get married before they had children. Crime did not pay, but hard work definitely did. People knew the difference. Moms could cook, Dads would work and sweat it out in the industries that bellowed and billowed smoke into the environment. People did not know anything about the negative effects brought by the destruction of the ozone layer.

The effects of climate change as well as that of gases emitted into the atmosphere by greenhouses were unheard of, neither were they thought of. Children then would behave. They would strive to walk the long, narrow and straight path charted by their parents.

Children then would not dabble in drug trafficking. Children then never thought of being involved in teenage prostitution. Genuine children would not engage in group sexual orgies.

They would not defile their bodies by having a plethora of tattoos engraved and emblazoned all over their bodies including the most sensitive and private of all parts.

Children would not always be high on drugs like *marijuana, mandrax, nyoape, heroine, chikwadzi, makodheni* and histallix. Children would not be *kubatwa nemushonga, kubatwa nezvinhu, kurekenwa, kutatamurwa*.

Teenage girls would not compete to lose their virginity. Teenage boys would not compete to impregnate teenage girls in the community. Teenage girls would then not pawn their virginity for any smart phone especially iPad and iPhone. Teenagers would not compete to transmit nude pictures on the social media. Teenagers would not engage in threesomes.

Teenage girls would not date men old enough to be their grand pas. Teenage boys, the Ben Tens would not compete for affection from sugar mamas, women old enough to be their grannies.

Most teenage boys who are lazy now spend most of their time googling, stalking and scrolling for dating sites with a view to get hooked to effluent and opulent sugar mamas who would spoil them with good lives. Teenagers then would direct their energies to make their parents and God happy.

Now teenagers spend the largest chunk of their productive time glued on blue movies, just to make their older sexual partners happy in bed. Teenage girls were more worried about losing virginity outside wedlock, now teenage girls are worried about where to get morning pills after some sexual jaunts.

It was taboo for teenage girls to fall pregnant outside wedlock. Teenage girls now use pregnancy as bait to lure sugar daddies to a perceived blissful life. Husbands then were loving, wives supportive and faithful.

Husbands and wives now compete to outfox each other in bed. They are no longer content with their lifetime sexual partners. They compete to infect each other with sexual transmitted infections. They compete for the leading role in the house. Wives are now more faithful to their boyfriends than husbands. Most wives' private parts are no longer private. They have gone commercial and are now competing with teenage girls in running parallel markets.

Children were polite. Now children are swaggerish, walk with a swagger for a gait, teenage boys stroll the streets with exposed pants, tattooed bums and raised collars. Teenage girls now wander the streets with deliberately exposed cleavage, are adorned with a myriad of rings, nose rings, navel rings, tongue rings on tongues that spew spleen, chilling candidness and unprintable words. In their walk of shame, they parade their God given wares to any man who would be up to the bargain.

Most children are no longer polite, but dabble in homosexual acts, acts perpetrated and perpetuated by individuals that our visionary and principled President described as worse off than pigs and dogs. Most children are no longer sure of their sexual orientation.

CHAPTER 17

SIGNS OF THE TIMES

Women wore dresses and men wore trousers. Now women wear men's trousers more than men themselves do. Women drink beer and smoke more than men. Women now attend and frequent wild parties more than men.

Women are now more daring and adventurous than men. Women always enjoy it whenever they throw caution to the wind. Women then looked like ladies, men like gentlemen and children looked decent.

People then loved the truth as it always set them free, they hated lies. The truth no longer sets people free, but bind them forever, for if the truth is revealed many marriages will be put asunder. If the truth is revealed, men and women would lose elections, respect and statuses.

Men and women are surviving on lies that have been told repeatedly with chilling accuracy and consistency. Then people came to church to get IN, Not to get OUT, that is to be saved and not to be served.

The church was a House of God, now it is a House of Men. The church belonged to God, now they belong to Men. God laid claim to all Earthly churches, but now some Men now lay claim to churches. Pastors would preach salvation, now prophets and prophetesses preach only about breakthroughs, deliverance and prosperity. The only known Prophetess in the Bible was Annah, now wives of self-proclaimed prophets have all become prophetesses.

Prophetesses in title not in the spiritual realm. Prophetesses who have never prophesied to any congregant, but nobody has dared to challenge them for they have been hegemonesed, *Touch Not the Anointed.*'

Hymns sounded Godly then, but now they sound Earthly, secular and heathen. Hymns glorified God then, now hymns gratify Men. Sermons sounded helpful then, now sermons sound sensational, confusing and laced with hate jibes aimed at perceived rival ministries or sects.

Rejoicing sounded normal and crying sounded sincere. Rejoicing now sounds abnormal and sensationalised. Crying now sounds rehearsed.

Demons manifested and were exorcised using the power of God. Now some demons are choreographed, manifestations stage-managed and exorcised through the powers of the *Prince of Demons*.

Testimonies were inspiring then, awesome, unbelievable, never doubted, were not sensationalised to hero worshipping, curry flavoured, laced with wheedling or simply meant to bootlick or glorify the Men of God.

Congregants or those who claim to have been healed from some chronic ailments, or received some life changing breakthroughs would narrate their testimonies with a passion carefully glorifying the man of God. Cursing was wicked, drinking was evil and divorce was unthinkable. Cursing is now sustained. Drinking has become fashionable.

Divorce is now the most desired and sought after solution by married couples who would have become incompatible, whose marriage would have become irretrievably broken down.

We read the Bible in public and prayed in school. Now financially constrained beer gardens have closed shop to pave way for churches and some loss making churches have been turned into schools.

Loss making churches? But are churches supposed to be money making ventures? Founders of churches or ministries, *vatumwa* will tell you that churches or ministries are not moneymaking entities whenever they want to escape from the taxman's noose.

But actions, extravagance, opulence, affluence and sometimes arrogance synonymous with some of these founders of ministries will point to the perception that churches have become big businesses worldwide. And indeed most of them have. No wonder why the largest chunk of founders of these ministries that have proliferated over the years, are listed among their countries' richest personalities.

That has led to questions being raised about their motives or rather *integrities*, whether some of them are *Men of God or Gold*.

Whenever somebody appears to be stepping onto the toes of these *men of God*, or interrogating their business ethics or conducts, they would be quickly reminded to *Touch Not the Anointed*, widely viewed as a veiled attack. Preachers would preach the word from house to house like

Jehova's Witnesses then. Being called a Christian was worth living for anyone who claimed to follow Christ Jesus. Judge not for you not to be judged.

Sex was a personal word. Homosexual was a word that was unheard of and abortion was an illegal word. Preachers preached because they had a message, but now preachers take turns to preach along town streets just to entertain street vendors, street urchins and desperate job seekers who would be too gullible to swallow any solution hook, line and sinker.

The preachers would be competing amongst themselves just to see who woos the most number of listeners. They do not compete to see who amongst themselves wins the largest number of souls for Christ, for their own souls are corrupted by their insatiable love for money and earthly riches. Maybe they have messages. Christians rejoiced because they had the *Victory!* Now Christians rejoice because they enjoy a political freedom that allows them to enjoy Freedom of Worship, they rejoice because they have the liberty to show the sign of *Victory!*

Preachers preached from the Bible, preachers preached the word not the world. Singers sang from the heart, not loudly in praise of the founder for their supper. Praise and Worship singers no longer sing from the heart for the Lord, they now sing with a passionate heart for the prophet, pastor.

They sing some corrupted secular songs with a passion. Sinners turned to the Lord to be *SAVED!* The poverty-stricken now turn to prophets and pastors to be delivered from spirits of poverty.

Poverty is a spirit. Those who wallow in abject poverty are told by prophets. But didn't Christ Jesus die a poor man, who was worse off than foxes that have holes?

Laws were based on the Bible not doctrine of the ministry, church or sect. Homes read the Bible and churches taught the Bible. Preachers were more interested in new converts than latest designer suits, multi-coloured outfits and top of the range fuel guzzlers.

At the church was where you found Christians on the Lord's Day, rather than in the parks, on the creek banks, golf courses, movie houses or being entertained somewhere else. The world was not as under siege from the devil as it is.

CHAPTER 18

BRAGGING RIGHTS

After the feast that annually marked Christmas festivities, church members would sing themselves hoarse.

At the crack of dawn, members of the Premier Harvest Pentecostal Assembly in which Baba was an evangelist would troop out to their homes where they would celebrate the day in various ways as dictated by the Bible.

My family used to stay at a clubhouse at Fern Valley Dam where my father was employed as a caretaker with a social club, which was a preserve for whites. It was strictly for members only.

He was in charge of some oar-propelled boats, which were used during fishing competitions. Lest we forget, Fern Valley, which is in Mutare off the Mutare-Masvingo highway, was a white community.

Blacks who lived in that area were those employed as domestic workers by the white minority, those employed as garden boys and nannies.

The inferiority complex ran so deep among black Rhodesians that most women would go through a lot of pains and sacrifices just to have a lighter skin. Then having a lighter skin pigment was the in thing just like what it is today.

So fashionable was it that African women with a lighter skin pigment were on high demand among lustful and corrupted African men. That explains why the Krol twins Sol and Abel made a fortune through the sale of skin lightening creams.

Back then and decades of years before, black migrant workers from Rhodesia would bring home light-skinned *baSotho* ladies to show off to their homeboys.

These uncles of ours would go to great lengths to impress their queen of hearts with their hard earned money from mines dotted in the Witwatersrand.

In most cases, they would come home with nothing to show for their toil and sweat, but a handful of some unique umbrellas, which could be converted into chairs on which they would sit as they take, rests along the great trek back home.

The other thing they would bring home were bragging rights. '*KuJoni tinodai or taidai.*' They wanted to do things differently from their contemporaries in the community then.

They would not stoop so low as to share *doro remasese, or fodya yechimonera.* They would go places to purse those lips as they bellowed and smoked from a pipe. That earned those nicknames like *Mujubheki or Mapaipi.*

Despite having brought almost nothing home, but doctored tales of success, romantic tales spiced with adventures of how they would have fought and defeated hands down some Zulu societal misfits in compassionate duels, they still had the magic to turn and sway infatuated and passionate dozens of female heads in the village. The *Mujubhekis* and *Mapaipis* possessed the *Midas touch.* Everything they laid their hands on would change to gold.

Regardless of the number of female heads they turned in their communities, the *Mujubhekis* would always shed a tear or two behind tongues of grotesque shadows. They would shed a tear or two of migration.

Under those raga blankets, lonely and yearning for the warmth and caressing dainty hands of their *baSotho* women. Women who were quick to file for divorce or terminate their unions with black Rhodesian men who would have been exhausted both romantically, sexually and physically. Under those blankets, tears of migration as well as tears of frustration would cascade down the wrinkle infested faces of the *Mujubhekis.*

They would have been told clearly to leave children born during the subsistence of their cohabitation period. What they would brood over during those lonely nights were faint memories of their happier times. Times when everything appeared to be rosy and a stroll in the park, they would behave as if they did not have any relatives back in Rhodesia, as if their relatives were trash and deserved to be treated with contempt and disdain.

Some would abandon their wives and children back home once they set their foot in *Egoli* where they were lured by the allure of bright red lights that are synonymous with the skyscrapers of Johannesburg. They would toil and break a sweat, which they would wipe away with their crowns.

There the *Mujubhekis* and *Mapaipis* who would have developed a predilection for expensive life styles and lighter skinned ladies, would fend for their girlfriends' offspring whilst back home their children and wives would shed tears of migration.

To the progressive ones, we would sing praise songs repeatedly, '*Mumwe murume akaenda Jubheki, kunotenga bheri bhotomu yake. Pakudzoka akadzoka nemota, mota yacho pio pio pijoti.*' That was a song passed onto us from the early 60s into the 70s.

Why would they occasionally shed tears of migration? Some of their contemporaries would tell them straight in their faces, of how they would have failed to change the face of the villages they hailed from with their airs. Bragging addictions. Bragging was like an opium of our people, those that had migrated. It appeared then that bragging was so contagious, that disease seemed to have inflicted only those who had skipped our borders.

CHAPTER 19

LIKE A PRAYER

Legend had it that all boys had to do was to mark a *Mubvee* fruit that had the size of a manhood of their choice or rather desire. The problem that arose with such prescriptions as we were told then was that there had to be a point when that *Mubvee* fruit had to be chopped or weaned off from her mother.

Failure, the menhoods would develop to astronomical levels that would scare away women. That would only happen when the *Mubvee* fruit was forgotten and allowed to grow naturally, so says the legend.

During baths at the river, we would compare and contrast our menhoods. We would exchange notes on courtship. We would engage in explicit lyrics competition. We would engage in explicit verbal duels. We would pleasure ourselves.

That was how we would pass on time as we suffered from hydrophobia. We hated bathing with a passion then. There we would take our time to restore our appearances that would have been overtaken with the passage of time.

We would smear our bodies with a plethora of jellies like *Mafutalin, Shell, American Girl, Bintu,* or even *Ambi,* a version of diproson, an outlawed skin enlightener and Ponds that we would have pinched from our sisters. Older boys, who would have been sauntering on the courting age, would stretch their afro hair using some red-hot bathing stones that would have been blast furnaced on the river banks. After that, they would apply not hair oil, but cooking oil, *mafuta enzungu,* just to give that hair of them a shiny appeal.

An appeal that would make them appear like some foreign super stars that they would have seen in some gloss and scented magazines. Some of our less fortunate sisters would sugar coat their legs so that they would have an edge over other community girls.

Some teenage girls from poverty reeking families, who could not afford to buy some makeup kits, would apply ground red bricks on their faces as face powder. I still vividly remember then that Amai used to give each one of use a cake of soap to use for a week. She would also dole to each one of us an equal portion of Vaseline jelly. Amai would always complain of how careless Sisi Runiya was with soap and Vaseline jelly.

She would smear the jelly all over her body including her nails. As if that was not enough wastage, she would use foamed water for bathing. Whenever Sisi Runiya ran out of her soap and Vaseline supplies, she would apply cooking oil.

CHAPTER 20

SEARCH WARRANT

But then we had to be very careful with Sisi Runiya by hiding our ration where she would not stumble upon. But then Sisi Runiya was something I must say. She would sniff out our rations without breaking a search warrant, without breaking a sweat as if she dabbled in *mishonga yekunyumwa, minyumwa nyumwa*. Everyone thought she used a hyena's nose when it came to sniffing out.

At the river, we would comb straight our afro hair which usually went unkempt for months despite the ever presence of afro-combs that dangled from our heads. Sometimes we would leave some furrows on the sides of our heads.

That style that was synonymous with most elders of Malawian origin was known in the hairdressing parlance as *dharakisheni*. Back then, that hairstyle was both stylish and fashionable. Some of our contemporaries would comb their afro hair backwards into *pushbacks*.

At times, we would have our hair trimmed leaving a small portion of the hair cropping out at the centre of the head extending to the forehead. That style was known back then as *bhibho*. After getting our hair done, we would then roam, stroll, patrol and prowl the hood with towels dangling around our swarthy necks. Patrolling of the hood whilst an afro comb stuck out in an unkempt head was a fashion statement.

We would use saliva to wipe away dust picked up whilst playing plastic balls from dusty fields or worse still, we would use blankets to get rid of that dust that would have stuck to us like leeches.

There were very few to warrant wrestling contests that were usually punctuated by spills of tears, a running nose and trickling of blood during most nights. Times without number, I had witnessed my elder brothers wrestling over blankets.

On times too many to be enumerated, I had witnessed wars erupting over the control of blankets. I was fortunate enough not to have been involved in those battles of superiority as tradition always demanded then that the youngest amongst the siblings would sleep in the middle.

That middle position meant the youngest siblings would be exempted or rather saved from the blushes of those titanic clashes that usually involved the seniors who were naturally muscular and tactically superior and smarter. Sometimes we would spend most nights warming up or rekindling dying ambers of fires as we battled to keep ourselves warm from the biting cold. I remember one day how after failing to withstand the sight of my elder siblings fighting over blankets, I had unsuccessfully tried to put up in a big homemade *masowe* crafted dish full of warm water. I only watered out or rather dripped out of the water after it had lost its warmth. I was obviously drugged with foolishness and youthfulness. How I hated bedtime then. How I wished I were born in a middle class family that could afford to incentivize their children.

How I envied some of our contemporaries who hailed from better off families especially teachers, British South African police officers and nurses. These would only agree to be bathed after a slice of bread spread with margarine would have been dangled before them.

We, who hailed from families that were afflicted with abject poverty, were not incentivized to take our baths. Our families just could not afford such.

CHAPTER 21

DAYS OF OUR LIVES

At the river, a tributary of Dora River we would stretch our hair, as we would be at pains to look like our western heroes. Satisfied with our appearances, we would trudge home where new clothes awaited us.

We would put on our perfectly ironed clothes with matching *Tenderfoot* tennis shoes, *Superpro* shoes, *Tomy* tennis, *Maripoza* and the fortunate ones would sport *Superstars*. *Superstars* were there before the advent of *Northstars* and *Addidases*.

We would then ample lackadaisically to Mudhara Joromiya who owned the most sophisticated and expensive gramophone in the black community. Mudhara Joromiya who was childless had spent the larger part of his youthful years in Johannesburg where he earned a fortune.

Apart from earning respect among members of the community, he had also earned a nickname *Mujubheki*. He was married to the most beautiful and lightest skinned lady in the community, a *baSotho* whom he had imported from South Africa.

We would call her Ambuya Mukaradhi, the coloured one. I later learnt how jealousy struck *Mujubheki* was. A plethora of kangaroo courts was assembled by lustful men from the community who would scheme on means and ways of luring his wife, Ambuya Mukaradhi to bed.

CHAPTER 22

THE BAIT

Those who would have managed to bait her to bed would share their experiences with other lustful men from the community. Those who would have won her heart, would brag about how lighter skinned her thighs, boobs and bums were.

Those who would have managed to sway her heart away from *Mujubheki*, would swank to their mates how good she was between the sheets. There others who would have had canal knowledge of Ambuya Mukaradhi would praise her for being an expert in bed.

Those were the days of gonorrhoea and syphilis. Those were the days when those infected would move around the community with legs astride and in excruciating pain.

Ambuya Mukaradhi who was generous by nature, would offer us plenty of food and beverages like carbonated drinks Coca Cola and Fanta as the *Wezhiras* would refer it to. Some offers, we would gladly grab and others we would turn down. Those whose offers we would have turned down would persuade us just to have a sample in the hope of whetting our taste buds. They would say '*Huyayi mudye vanangu ndezvepaChristmas, hazvirambwi.*'

Turning down food offers was taboo. It was just unheard of and unimaginable on Christmas day. The community then would offer food or even those delicacies you can think of freely, even to those they hated to the footprint. No child would be given a spanking by their parents for straying from the family pot, *kukwata*.

Those gestures would be extended even to the likes of Torpedo who was notorious for feeding into other families' pots. He would not wait to be invited over for food. He would simply deep his hands in the dirty brown water that would have been used to wash hands by family members. Then the entire family would wash their hands in the same dish using the same water.

He would always pay us visits whenever meals were accompanied by good relish. '*Anonyumwa kunge bere*,' we would say whilst resigning everything to fate. Whenever he visited, he would live us hungry.

He was not the type who would join you and withdraw before the plates were empty taking into consideration that his share awaited him at home. We would then mock him by imitating the humming of a certain species of birds.

That was Torpedo for you and Enjura was his elder sister who walked with a limp having succumbed to polio at a tender age. Apart from that handicap, Enjura was a beautiful girl blessed with some dimples.

I would like to believe that Enjura could have been the reason why Bhudhi Masango seemed to have a soft spot for Torpedo despite his well-documented food poaching misdemeanours. Bhudhi Masango, who we suspected could have been flirting with Enjura, would always defend Torpedo's actions to the hilt whenever we tore into him with reckless abandon.

He would always threaten to turn his coat by supping with the devil that was Mai Enjura and her live-in boyfriend Farashishiko who was of Mozambican extraction.

The duo were notorious for their nocturnal nature of business, which was necromancy and wizardry. Legend had it that whoever dared to cross their paths which were labyrinth in nature, would not live to tell tales of another day.

Even Amai, who was notorious for bad mouthing other people from the community, would always exercise restraint whenever an issue involved Farashishiko and his girlfriend Annasitenziya, Amai Enjura. However, I still vividly recall how Amai threw caution to the wind one night after some mysterious flying birds known in the underworld vernacular as zvishiri or zvivanda struck me. I was hallucinating and spewing obscenities in a strange voice that matched that of Annasitenziya.

My voice was not computer morphed or mutated to sound like Annasitenziya's, it was the nocturnal world that was at play. Even the application of *Tokoloshi* salt could not drive away the tormenting spirits. When Amai realised that I was sauntering towards the graveyard, she stormed outside with Baba in a lug, climbed an anthill that grotesquely cast out a tongue that longed for a kiss.

CHAPTER 23

HOUSE OF HELL

That tongue cast an evil shadow towards the *House of Horror*, a *House of Hell* that resembled a super highway to hell. Once she reached the pinnacle, she spewed unprintable words aimed at Farashishiko and Annasitenziya reproducing the very words I had been uttering in a trance-like state.

This action was known in the traditional circles as *kurova bembera*, whereby a villager goes on a tirade against their known and perceived enemies. Usually this was done after that person would have got wind of who would be tormenting them or their families in the supernatural world.

Once that was done, the tormentor would swiftly soften their hearts because the entire community would have been informed of who the perpetrator or tormentor was. Words travel far and wide during the night and worse still when broadcast from an anthill.

By climbing on an anthill was just as good as challenging wizards and witches to an open war. It would mean that if ever the person being afflicted by those who dabble in supernatural powers were to die and got interred on an anthill, they would be held accountable. After Amai's disparaging and too revealing siege at the duo, I drifted into normalcy. The only crime that I had committed was to have taken Torpedo to the cleaners with a tongue-lashing of his young life.

He had tried to trade back in the tongue-lashing contest, but found himself on the back foot. After failing to match my inflaming tongue, he had broken into an uncontrolled snivel that was punctuated with a deluge of tears and hiccups that threatened to choke him.

Having dismally lost the verbal tirade of a duel, Torpedo had trudged home under the weight of a heavy and bleeding heart. When he got home, under bursts of sniffles, he had poured his troubled heart to his heartless mother.

Legend had it that Annasitenziya swiftly drifted into a trance, summoned her *Airforce, zvishiri* which she sent to strike me with a barrage and myriad of *bombs* that left me paralysed and deranged. As they say, the rest is history.

If it were today, I would have been bundled into a vehicle and wheeled to Prophet Magaya's Prophetic Healing and Deliverance, for exorcism.

I would have been protected then had I been in possession of anointed mantles like anointing oil, wrist bands, scoops of soil from the Holy Ground or just a mere book like *Mweya Yemumvura*.

CHAPTER 24

SUPER SUPPER

The oldest brother or sister would be accorded the right to pick and choose from chunks of meat. If the most senior member delayed to land their chunk, the rest of the members would have to make do with soup.

We would eat from the same plate then like what Jesus Christ did during the Last Supper with his disciples.

That brought unity and respect amongst siblings. But then there were some members who would spoil the sea of soup by leaving a trail of remnants of morsels as if they would be out to lay bait on fish.

Once the sadza got finished, Amai would start to prepare another pot of sadza whilst we held tightly to our chunks of meat in readiness for another round of assault on the staple food.

Then poultry meat from indigenous chickens then had a lot of importance attached to them. The drum sticks, gizzards, and feet would be served to the head of the house, Baba.

Failure to observe that law would result in wives being sent packing to their parents. Legend has it that in some households all gizzards of chickens slaughtered during the absence of that household's head would be all dried and kept in the kitchen for him. Nobody would be served with those. The backbone was a preserve for Amai and only intestines, heart, wings, neck and head would be left for the children.

I vividly recall how my two nieces and I used to haggle and grapple over the right to serve Baba his supper which in most cases would have been conserved in a lidded food container with handles, popularly known then as *dheka*.

We would watch him wash one hand of his. Incongruously Baba would not allow us to do the same as he reckoned that only those who would have lost one of their parents could afford to wash one hand before eating. We would stand guard as he consumed his food, following the movements of his hand as he surreptitiously ate his food.

We would also open our mouths whenever he shoved morsels of food into his salivating mouth.

We knew very well that he would leave some meat and sadza for whoever would have served him. That gesture was tantamount to a tip like those usually extended to workers in the tourism industry.

We would rejoice then, whenever a visitor paid us a courtesy call. The reason being that, a chicken would have to be slaughtered as per tradition then. Whilst everyone would be happy to have a taste of poultry or white meat, Bhudhi Maikoro would be shedding a deluge of tears of migration.

CHAPTER 25

THE PAIN OF MIGRATION

'Nhai imi babamunini, munoenda riini kumba kwenyu makutipedzera nyama yedu, asi hamuna kumba kani?'

In most cases, relatives who would be asked to leave or worse indirectly served with eviction notices by these *uncouth children* would be from the paternal side.

The fact that all relatives who would be up for eviction or deportation would be from the paternal side, spoke volumes of the mothers of those children's hatred towards their husbands' relatives.

Bhudhi Maikoro would be shedding tears in memory of one of his birds that would end up as part of the family dish.

Tradition then demanded that once that chicken was prepared, it would be taken to the visitor who would be accorded the honour to dish it out. Usually it would be prepared in a clay pot, *hadyana* and spiced with very small tomatoes known as *maturuzha*.

There had to be two dishes, one for the visitor or visitors and the other one for the family consumption should the visitors decide to have the whole poultry dish to themselves, which was rare then. Bhudhi Maikoro, who was a brilliant student, owned all the chickens that roamed our yard.

Everytime he came out tops at Sheni Primary School in Dangamvura, Amai would give him a chick to incentivise him. As years moved by, those chicks would grow into hens that would lay eggs, hatch chicks that they would raise.

That's how he came to lay claim to all the chickens that we kept. Just to provoke him, we would ask Amai that we yearned for poultry meat.

Although the family owned many domesticated rabbits, a few would clamour and bay for their blood. Only Bhudhi Masango would relish the slaughtering of those rabbits.

The reason being that it was him and Baba who would feast on the meat, which he would have dried and spiced with hot chillies. He would pull out a rabbit from the rabbit pen, armed himself with a hammer, which he would use to strike the rabbit on the forehead sending its eyes popping out of their sockets.

Mother would then use the largest pot in the kitchen to prepare the family's sadza whenever sadza was to be accompanied with good relish.

Only a few families could afford to have lunch accompanied with a special dish, *sadza nenyama*. Then most parents could not afford to provide three descent meals a day. Most mothers would delay the family breakfast so that it coincided with lunch.

We would not wash our hands after a super supper so that we would crow about to our friends. We would calculatingly leave some traces of soup crossing through our legs that we would have not washed for days on end. We would leave out chewed remains of meat hanging between our teeth just to prove to all and sundry that we would have had meat for relish, just to settle scores with our contemporaries.

CHAPTER 26

SONGS OF OUR TIME

Mudhara Mujubheki's place would always be teeming with joy seekers or party animals. Mudhara Mujubheki would stack vinyl records on his gramophone, which would automatically remove the vinyl record that would have been played unless by encore, *hengoooooo*, that was by public demand.

A coin or two would be placed on top of the gramophone's head to enable the stylus to sail through scratches on vinyl records without hiccups.

To minimize scratches on vinyl records, methylated spirit was used as a cleaning agent. When days were dark then, those addicted to the bottle would turn to methylated spirit as a substitute for alcohol.

To lessen its effects on their health, those who dabbled in intoxicants, would strike a few matchsticks, which they would throw, into the bottle as they sought to weaken its alcoholic effects.

Africans then were not allowed to imbibe in bottled alcohol. Blacks would converge in community beer halls where they would drown their sorrows with opaque beer, which used to be served in large white beer mugs. In Mutare, blacks would converge at *Murapa, Chidzere, Maonde, Mushando, paChigomba* to mention, but a few.

Music would blare from jukeboxes. Some bullies would not allow anyone to dance to music they would have paid for to be played on the jukebox.

I can vividly recall songs like *Simon Agira, Rozallina Soda, Sellina, Small Time No10, 17 Mabone, Jumbo Jet, Connie, Anopenga, Ane Waya, Aphiri Anabwera, Vakadzi Varume, varikubva Jubheki* to mention, but a few. Most of those songs from South Africa's *Simanje manje* genre were instrumental.

Creative as we were, we would coin lyrics to suit our sing-along appetites from Oliver Mtukudzi and Thomas Mapfumo. Other artistes like Zexie Manatsa also made their presence felt on the showbiz circles.

Safirio Madzikatire and son Elijah, Tinei Chikupo, the Harare Mambos, the Hurricanes, Spokes Mashiane, the Beatles, Jimi Hendrix, Job Mashanda, Jonah Moyo and the Devera Ngwena Jazz Band and others too numerous to mention, also stole our hearts.

With the advent of *uhuru* came a flurry of new bands, new artistes like Mashanda, The Bhundu Boys, Rozalla Miller, Marshall Munhunumwe, Tobias Ariketa, James Chimombe, Sunrise Kwela Kings, Zimbabwe Clear Sounds, David Ziome who led the Zimbabwe Chachacha Kings, Sebastian and Stanely Manatsa and the Rusikes also burst onto the scene. Mandebvu, the Runn Family, the Moses Marasha and David Mapfuwamhandu propelled Nyaminyami Sounds, Hurungwe Sounds and Paul Matavire to mention, but a few also arrived on stage to stake their claim on the showbiz scene.

CHAPTER 27

OF ILLICIT BREW AND NIGHT CRAWLERS

Those were the days of *Society Tea Parties* where alcoholic beverages and traditional brew were also sold to revellers and night crawlers. Soft drinks and foods were served and also sold at inflated prices as communities battled to fundraise for *mukando, bharoni* or *round*.

Music then would only be played upon special request. That request had a monetary value attached to it. The gramophones, which then were status symbols, were a preserve for just a few.

Those who owned them would have acquired them from auctions. The majority then owned smaller ones like Supersonic and WRS, which were shaped like some briefcases.

To boost or amplify their sound output, their owners would place them on top of small drums or water cans. These *Society Tea Parties* sauntered into the early 90s where they were later overtaken by events.

In my rural home of Mt Darwin, some enterprising Society Parties hosts among them Mudhara Toperesu would fence off his yard using grass thatch, the same used on *chinjausi*. He would then bring home from Madondo and Dotito, a truckload of flesh peddlers who he would have hired to provide passionate companionship to joy seekers.

Mudhara Toperesu would get into a pact with flesh peddlers who would service clients for a fee that would leave both parties smiling all the way to the bank.

Having danced the Christmas' night away, we would stay indoors until the sun was up there, *pagumi nembiri*. We would move around our community scrounging for leftovers from the previous day.

We would feast on bread that would have been left to dry in the sisal bowls. Bread then would be purchased in dozens. Households would compete to see who would buy the most number of dozens. We would dip the dried slices of bread into our cups of tea.

We would turn the community upside down in search of goodies that we would have ignored the previous day.

We would ask for *Kirisimasi bhokisi* from close and distant relatives who cared to listen and respond.

Some of the responses would be, '*Nyarara zvako ndichakuuraira huku nekukutengera kokokora nemabhanzi,*' depending on the relationship that would be prevailing between the speakers. The poverty-stricken community then would resort to preparing dishes with Holsum or Dripping, some cheaper grade cooking fat that came in the solid form like margarine.

When eating a relish prepared with that form of cooking fat, one had to be close to a fire to keep the plate on hot ambers to prevent solidification. That fat would require warm water to wash hands with, as it would stick around leaving a real mess. Poor families would also resort to cheaper household baskets like coarse salt, brown bread and brown sugar.

We would flock to the Fort Victoria-Umtali, Melsetter highway where we would stake claim to passing traffic. We would claim to ourselves the Mercedes Benzes, Zodiacs, Zephyrs, Peugeot 404s, Morris Minors, VW Beetles, BMW Cheetahs, Austin Cambridges and Land Rovers. Toyota Crowns, Foden trucks, Daf and buses that belonged to Chinyarishoko, Chingaira, Siduna, Msabaeka and the United Passsenger Company wheeled past the road.

As soon as the Christmas holidays limped to the finishing tape, the society would return to normal. Food would no longer be offered to passers. Food would be whisked away from the glare of visitors upon hearing the pattering of footsteps.

As food supplies continued to peter out, the community would revert to descending on errant children especially those who would have strayed and preyed on other families' pots. Suddenly the community would resort to drinking traditional *mahewu* made from *sadza* and *chimera*. The elderly would spend their time in their fields as they would be pondering on what to dish out to their families on an entirely brand new holiday. A holiday that marked a countdown to a hectic journey, New Year. Christmas days then were days everyone looked to with zeal and zest. Even pagans held the holiday in high esteem.

Urbanites would leave their dwellings in droves and flocks for their rural areas. The day was treasured in the sense that it brought relatives together, relatives who would have last met the previous Christmas holiday.

Siblings who would have last converged the previous Christmas holiday to deliberate on the improvement of the family's homestead and most importantly, their parents' welfare, would assemble to embark on a postmortem of projects.

Sporadic running battles would break out between *home defenders* and urbanites over the jewels of the village, village belles. The home defenders, a derogatory term that refers to unemployed village youths, would be out to claim village belles to themselves, as they would have spent a fortune on them in the course of the year.

CHAPTER 28

THE TEST OF TIME

On the other hand, the village belles would be out to capitalize on their looks by hanging around with the urbanites who in most cases would be prepared to spend a fortune just to sway them from their long time lovers. Village beauties would also be out to weigh marriage options.

Those were the days when village girls would be quick to offer their hands in marriages upon being shown photographs or snaps of potential suitors, snaps of urbanites. Strangers, total strangers could marry without a shred of doubt through matchmakers, *gwevedzis*.

Surprisingly, most of those marriages have stood the test of time, are still intact in contrast to those who would have dated over a longer period of time.

Today's youths who claim to be living in a global village that has torn the moral fabric into shreds, now hook up through the social media.

The social media where a new breed of untrained, but daring and technologically sound young men and women are calling themselves citizen journalists. That is through *Facebook* and *WhatsApp*, the equivalence of snaps and *gwevedzis*. Battles of supremacy would also be fought pitting the urbanites and those who would have migrated to South Africa. The two groups would fight it out for the hearts of the fairer sex as well as over bragging rights, '*KuHarare tinodai, kwaMutare tinodai, kuJoni tinodai,*'

There were also battles, family feuds fought to even scores of a battle that would have been fought and dismally lost the previous Christmas holiday.

Those battles, which usually fought away from the admonishing glare of the adult eye, were fought at business centres like Dande Storo, Chividze, Kajokoto, Dotito, Pachanza, Pfunyanguwo, Zambezi, Kanyoka, Nyamhepo, Mudzengerere in my rural area of Mt Darwin and her environs.

There, those battles would sometimes turn ugly, as fighters would resort to using an array of weapons at their disposal. Most of those wars were mostly won on numerical advantage and bravery than fighting prowess.

As years went by, those who fanned and partook in those brawls, would join sprouting martial arts clubs where they would perfect their fighting skills, which they would display on Christmas Day.

So important were the Christmas holidays that people would go to great lengths to invest so much in a day that comes once a year. People would go to the extent of borrowing clothes, designer suits just to create a lasting impression.

The Christmas holiday euphoria would force people to engage in impulse buying, a practice that would allow a fertile breeding ground for a virus that caused the *January Disease*. Then *majoni-joni* would save their hard-earned rands in order to hire a state of the art vehicle, which they would cruise around the village in, just to sweep away the heart of that village beauty single or married woman. Those were the days when the Christmas holiday fever could be detected in the air. So strong was the euphoria that we would almost caress and embrace it as those drugged with infatuation love do.

The euphoria was soft to the touch and yet smooth as a parrot's breast. Christmas holidays have over the years lost their flare, gloss, glitz, glamour, glitter and lustre.

Over the years, Christmas holidays have become too mediocre, too pathetic and too ordinary. The world over, the day has become too ordinary to be celebrated. What is now left are its fragmented memories, memories which are just too, too good to forget. No matter how good those memories can be, we just cannot turn back the hands of time, we just cannot turn back the years.

All we are able to do as contemporaries is to relive those jolly old, good days as we reminisce and take a walk down memory lane.

CHAPTER 29

MERCHANT OF DEATH

As years flirted by, our family moved to where Joubert Crushers currently is. Baba had just resigned from his job at the Fern Valley Dam after several runs in with his employers who he alleged were racists.

At one time, he was arrested by the then Ian Smith led government's police officers after he had lashed at three daughters of the Bothas who were riding on their father's horses.

The trio who had been petrified to the bone by Baba's actions, had ploughed through their family gate leaving it into a corrupted heap as they frantically tried to make good their escape from the raging African *boy* known also as *kaffir*.

Baba had been angered by the fact that the trio had earlier on unleashed their dogs on Sisi Garandichauya. The vicious dogs had ravaged and savaged her leaving her bloodied, clothes shredded and battling for what was left of her iota of life.

This sister of mine was something else. At one time, she had rounded up all the siblings and placed them in an oar-propelled boat before setting to sail off in the Fern Valley Dam in which a mermaid was said to have been on a prowl. After that gate-breaking incident, Baba was arrested and arraigned before the courts were charges of miscellaneous injury to property were leveled against him. He was convicted and slapped with a two-month custodial sentence that was later commuted to a fine. Extenuating circumstances that led to the commission of the crime were not taken into consideration since the pendulum of the law was heavily tilted in favour of white settlers. As the Second Chimurenga war rumbled on, so did the hatred that existed between Baba and the Fern Valley white community.

He had to call it quits after realizing that the strained relationship was not healthy for the family that had settled at Fern Valley Dam turning it into a sanctuary.

My family had relocated from Chipiso Village of Mt Darwin where the raging spirit of the Second Chimurenga was raving, ravaging, raging, ranting and threatening to consume villagers like a dinosaur.

Baba had landed a caretaker job with Baas Richard who had deserted his gazebo stylishly, that summerhouse near Joubert quarrying site just before Blue Desert and Madziro Butchery along the Mutare-Masvingo Highway.

We stayed there until around 1977 when the liberation war intensified. Baba had then secured a job with *Super Security* as a security sentinel. The security concern that was revered then could provide her staffers with some warm knee length coats like those usually sported by police officers during winter.

Ticket checkers with debt saddled National Railways of Zimbabwe used to don such long and heavy coats synonymous with the swish-swash sound. Apart from being issued with those coats, which were an envy to many, *Super Security* would also arm her guards with truncheons, security dogs and some red helmets.

The company treated premises as hardhat areas. Those hardhats had saved many a security guard's lives since many armed robbers would target to strike the head in a bid to incapacitate their victims.

All hell broke loose one fine night when the security firm resolved to arm Baba with an old-fashioned rifle known in African communities as *mubaya kamwe,* a gun that fired once, which he was supposed to use to scare away freedom fighters who used to come and sabotage Umtali Leather.

We advised Baba to resign from his job as a security guard forthwith as we genuinely felt that would put him in the line of fire.

The family unanimously agreed that doing so would be tantamount to putting Baba's head on the chopping block or guillotine.

Patriotic as we were, we felt allowing Baba to participate in a mission that would delay or derail our freedom, would be tantamount to betraying the raging spirit of the struggle. The founding principles or ethos of Chimurenga.

We believed that doing so would be equal to dicing with death or worse still a naïve and myopic attempt to bell the cat. We had a role to play in the liberation war, a war that had left our clan poorer as we had lost Bhudhi Tafirenyika and Babamunini Giribheti. Bhudhi Tafirenyika, whose nom de guerre was Cde Mabhunu Muchapera, was the leader of war collaborators in the Chipiso Village. He valiantly had to secure the release of his parents, Babamukuru Ginatsiyo and Amaiguru Jesimeni with his soul.

The Rhodesian Front whose soldiers were derogatorily referred to as *Mapuruvheya* conspiring with the *Skuzaapos*, had stumbled upon information that Bhudhi Tafirenyika had been receiving military training at a freedom fighters' base in the Chiswiti area. Skuzaapos were part and parcel of the Rhodesian Front forces who disguised as freedom fighters.

Bhudhi Tafirenyika also stood accused of having been instrumental in the recruitment of students and villagers into the freedom army.

Bhudhi Tafirenyika commanded great respect from students at Mavhuradonha Mission High School, Chigango Secondary School, Chiswiti High School, St Alberts, Bradley Institution, Pfunyanguwo High School and Mudzengerere High School among other institutions.

The RF desperately wanted to pick him up for interrogation. When the Mapuruvheyas marched into Babamukuru Ginatsiyo's homestead, Bhudhi Tafirenyika who we later gathered had been using a herbal concoction in which a vulture's head was a major component, had just slipped away right under the nemesis forces' noses. A vulture's head was believed to be used by many fake prophets as a paraphernalia during prophesying.

Prophets who dabble in it can even *prophesy* to the dot even national identity cards numbers, drivers' licenses numbers, vehicle registration plates, football results, major political events, deaths, births, sex of unborn babies, colour of clothes worn by your enemies and friends as well as dates on epitaphs.

Others use a hyena's nose. A hyena's nose also works in the same way as a vulture's head. Bhudhi Tafirenyika had managed to slice through the eagle eyed Rhodesian forces.

He had surprisingly managed to escape right under the antagonist's nose. The Mapuruvheyas' noses must have been too big for the occupants not to notice what was going on underneath them.

The Mapuruvheyas who had failed to close in on Bhudhi Tafirenyika for the third time in as many attempts, felt humiliated and had to drag Babamukuru Ginatsiyo and Amaiguru Jesimeni to their base at Mavhuradonha Mission School where they were keeping students under surveillance.

The Mapuruvheyas had vowed to release the pair if only Bhudhi Tafirenyika were to show up at their base.

CHAPTER 30

STRIDES OF BRAVERY

Bhudhi Tafirenyika had received news of what had befallen his parents and had to conduct some reconnaissance with the aid of the vulture's head, before returning home soon after darkness had grotesquely enveloped Chipiso Village.

The mood in the village was sombre. The village had been plunged into mourning. Villagers spoke in hushed voices punctuated with sobs of anger.

Sobs of oppression, sobs of freedom. Sobs of a revolution and sobs whose tears were dying to be wiped away by a consolatory hand. Sobs that fought a surging and bottled consternation from within. Sobs that yearned for independence.

They brooded over events that had taken place during that Friday the 13th. Bhudhi Tafirenyika was welcomed with sobs of trepidation and muffled cries for Babamukuru Ginatsiyo and Amaiguru Jesimeni.

After calm had returned, Ambuya Marujata had to order Bhudhi Tafirenyika to go and secure the release of his parents. Amid sobs, he bade everyone who was in attendance farewell before trudging out into the gloomy night.

Even though nearly forty years have passed, I vividly remember how he was reported to have had struggled to convince Ambuya Marujata, amid sobs that he would not make it out of Mapuruvheyas' dungeon of death alive.

But Ambuya Marujatawho could not come to terms with the gravity of losing a son and a daughter in-law, remained pig-headed. She just could not be convinced or rather moved.

She strongly believed that Bhudhi Tafirenyika would be released by the Mapuruvheyas after questioning. The Mapuruvheyas had impressed upon Ambuya Marujata with a myriad of assurances that they did not meant to harm Bhudhi Tafirenyika.

All they wanted from him was to assist them with their

investigations after which they would release him into the custody of his parents. But alas, that was not meant to be.

That night was the last those he had bade farewell in that dingy dining room had seen him alive. That was the very night Babamukuru Ginatsiyo and Amaiguru Jesimeni had seen him alive too.

He had gallantly marched into Mapuruvheyas fortified territory unarmed just to secure the release of his parents, who true to Mapuruvheyas' words, were freed into the dark village where phantoms prowled.

Legend has it that Bhudhi Tafirenyika was dangled to a high flying helicopter that later plunged him into the crocodile and hippo infested Zambezi River.

Legend also says that a rope that was tied to his feet was made to snap sending him plunging headlong into the deeper end of the vast mystic river. These are legends which are too ghastly to envisage and are also too many to fathom and digest.

Up to now, nobody knows where he was interred if at all, such an event took place. 'Prophets and spirit mediums' kept our hopes alive whenever the clan consulted them.

'He is still alive,' spirit mediums would tell us. 'One of these fine days, Bhudhi Tafirenyika will stride back home in military fatigue,' others would prophesy to us. But now we are pretty convinced that he is no more. He would never come to join us during family gatherings, but now awaits us in another life, somewhere.

For he lies somewhere at the Tomb *of the Unknown Soldier.* Somewhere in an unmarked grave, somewhere at the belly of the mighty Zambezi River.

CHAPTER 31

PLUNGED INTO MOURNING

Three months down the line, as the clan was still trying to come to terms with the fate of Bhudhi Tafirenyika, another catastrophe struck again.

Babamunini Giribheti was killed in a cross fire when freedom fighters and Skuzaapos traded fire at the midst of a village risking the lives and appendages of villagers who were imbibing the traditional brew at Nhamoyembwa.

Villagers had converged to drown their sorrows at the Nhamoyembwa in Kamutsenzere Village when fighting broke out sending beer guzzlers scurrying for cover.

What happened was that freedom fighters had gathered intelligence from some war collaborators that they were some Skuzaapos who had infiltrated the village posing as freedom fighters.

Among those Skuzaapos were white soldiers who had painted their faces, hair and hands black in a desperate bid to blend well with their fellow black servicemen.

It was their pointed noses, some white patches that remained at the back of their ears and their shiny eyes that had previously given them away.

The freedom fighters instructed occupants of the homestead the Skuzaapos had visited to dole them a lot of traditional beer to debilitate them. The guerrillas had also instructed villagers to lie prostrate or prone once their guns started to stutter and utter their messages of death. The freedom fighters who had laid an ambush around the homestead had warned villagers not to burst through their ambush. Anyone who dared to do so risked being gunned down as collateral damage.

As darkness blanketed the village, the freedom fighters carried out their operation as per strategy. A handful of villagers who were not privy to the goings on were taken aback by the new twist of events.

They had genuinely believed or had been hoodwinked into believing that the Skuzaapos were guerrillas. One hapless villager was Babamunini Giribheti.

Babamunini Giribheti who appeared to have had one too many as he staggered under Dutch courage, was not as lucky as he was caught by a hail of bullets that sent him mowing to the ground. Bloody gushed out in a crimson red fine spray.

He lay there writhing in agony, gasping for breath in paroxysms of pain as he frantically tried to stuff protruding intestines back into his stomach. He winced in great pain as he withdrew his hands that were soaked in blood.

He gave a loud cry that drowned the spluttering guns that were stuttering their messages of death. He breathed his last after he had given his last and laconic prayer in which he was asking his Maker to accommodate his soul.

Babamunini Giribheti was later picked up for traditional rites. His body had to lie in state at his homestead where friends, close relatives, children and wife wailed uncontrollably thereby cutting a tearful scene.

Freedom fighters and Skuzaapo blamed each other for the tragedy. 'We should not have exchanged gun fire in the midst of the village in the first place,' they reasoned.

Even if they threw around a plethora of scapegoats, which would never bring my beloved Babamunini Giribheti, the hilarious one back to life.

Even if they had owned up with the truth with regards to who should have been blamed for igniting the match that torched the battle that left a myriad of collateral damages in her trail, it would never bring our Babamunini Giribheti back to Chipiso Village.

Even if a Commission of enquiry to get to the bottom of the causative agents of the battle were to be constituted, Babamunini Giribheti would not come back from the dead.

A day later, Babamunini Giribheti was interred at the family graveyard where he was laid along his father Sekuru Hwamanda and great grandfather Ngororombe.

That sombre day that was pregnant with tears that cascaded freely down the cheeks of villagers, galvanised villagers into a regime change agenda.

When word filtered to us in Umtali that a hail of bullets had caught

Babamunini Giribheti, Baba resolved to visit Chipiso Village. He intended to pay his last respects to his younger brother as well as extending the family's condolence messages.

Baba failed to navigate his way to Chipiso as the road had been garlanded with landmines that made it virtually impassable.

CHAPTER 32

SPOILING FOR A FIGHT

We also felt that if Baba were to continue working for the District Administrator's wing, he would be derailing the revolutionary train's progress. The family also resolved to bury Baba's light hunter's rifle as it could be mistaken for an assault rifle by freedom fighters.

He later landed a job with the Williams who stayed in Fern Valley. The couple had fostered two sons Marshall and Mitchel. As the war intensified, the Williams relocated to the leafy Morningside low-density suburb, which was safer.

Struggling to take care of the large family, Baba abandoned us. He would come occasionally just to check on the family. He would ask us to submit a list of our educational needs and wants.

Whenever we supplied him with that list, he would spend months on end without honouring his commitment, let alone visiting us.

Deep down, we knew Baba had walked out on Amai and the entire family. None of us bothered to ask Amai the reason behind Baba's exit from the scene. Previously, we had witnessed them fighting fiercely. We had seen Amai nursing a black eye she would have picked up in a fistfight with Baba. She would lie to us that a bee would have stung her whenever we asked her what would have happened to her swollen eye. She was so protective of Baba so we all believed. She had been conditioned and stereotyped to suffer in silence. She had been brought up to accept a culture in which gender based violence was generally acceptable, accepted, condoned and perpetuated.

Or maybe she did not want to wash their dirty linen in public. Fights that would have started in the bedroom should have never filtered into the public domain.

Times without number we had watched Amai leaving for Baba's only Sister Tete Keresenziya who lived at a white owned farm in the then Hartley area now Chegutu.

Tete Keresenziya would then accompany Amai plus her luggage

back home where Tete would try to compel the duo to smoke the peace pipe.

Smoke the peace pipe the couple would do, but the effect of that smoke would not last long. Sooner than later, the pair would have wriggled out of the smoke of peace that would have engulfed and enveloped them.

Before Tete Keresenziya's footsteps would have been swept away by blowing winds and before we knew it, Amai would be tailing Tete Keresenziya to Hartley.

Another fight would have broken out between the warring couple who always blamed each other for breaching a verbal armistice that they would have entered into in the presence of Tete Keresenziya the peacemaker. After tripartite meetings to thrash some sticky points that would involve Baba, Tete and Amai, she would unpack her clothes from her suitcase as she hoped for a more tranquil environment.

Tete Keresenziya would sign off with, '*Basa ndasiya ndapedza,*' before being accompanied to *Musika weHuku* where she would fetch transport to her place of residence. Tete Keresenziya would only leave for her place of residence after feasting on more than two birds.

It appeared Tete Keresenziya was not a genuine peace broker. Mediators are not supposed to spend more time in the company of aggressors. She would spend more time in the company of Baba, her brother.

No wonder why she dismally failed to call to order Baba and Amai when they clashed over how Sisi Garandichauya's bride price was supposed to be shared between the two of them.

On that gruesome night, Amai who appeared hardened by several beatings she had endured at the hands of Baba, was determined to upstage the apple cart. She fought like a she tiger breaking Baba's arm in the process.

Before the fight escalated or got nastier or bloodier, she had to remove Baba's most prized wristwatch, the Oris which was purchased with proceeds from Sisi Garandichauya's bride price.

Ironically, Amai handed the Oris watch over to Sisi Garandichauya for safe keeping before warning Baba that she was spoiling for a *wafa wafa* sparing.

Unbeknown to Baba, Amai had learnt a trick or two of fighting back during previous encounters in which she had traditionally and submissively ended up getting the longer end of the stick.

That night was different from other nights in which she had lost without putting up a fight. Baba's arm had to be put in a plaster for it to mend. As the economic downturn worsened, fights escalated between our parents. Love had flown out of the window when poverty came stumbling, wobbling and knocking at the door like a nagging visitor.

We were left shedding tears and scars of domestic violence. Poverty was the source of those endless fights between our parents. Baba was out of employment leaving Amai to fend for the family.

Baba owned nothing save for himself. He possessed nothing except his name. He was worse off than a church mouse. Naturally, Amai would end up flexing her muscles, as she would be literally running the family show, dictating terms and conditions to Baba. She would refuse to take some orders from Baba who would vent off his anger and frustrations of being jobless by pummeling Amai into a bloody pulp. Amai would vow not to submit herself to Baba up and until he had taken over his fatherly role.

Till then, Baba had to stop preaching the *Head of the Family* gospel. Amai would mockingly challenge Baba to match his words with deeds and actions. '*Hubaba husina mabasa hwakafa. Hubaba hunotoshandirwa kwete nekupfeka mutaranginya asi nemabasa.*'

Sometimes Amai would get to the extent of serving Baba with sadza without meat when the rest of the family would be enjoying a super supper. Frustrated, Baba would fly into a rage, throwing some tantrums and just falling short of hurling some obscenities at Amai. Worse still, Amai would serve Baba's intended supper to the dogs.

But was it right to take the Head of the family's supper and throw it to the dogs? I used to wonder. Bhudhi Masango used to wonder, Bhudhi Maikoro wondered, Bhudhi Ranziroti wondered, Mukuwasha Furidhomu our brother-in-law wondered, so did the entire family. We all wallowed and waddled in wonderland. There was nothing we could do.

Our hands were tied. We too depended on Amai for survival. The least we could do was to share the little we would have been served together with Baba or better still join him on his forced hunger strikes.

Actions like those would attract tirades from Amai as well as some punitive measures that included the withdrawal of food rations. As time passed by, Amai began to see the light.

She began to take stock of her actions and resolved to reform. *Was it mere coincidence that Amai changed for the better when an under siege, lay wasted and pale Baba had literally taken to Mapositori for salvation and divine solutions?*

He genuinely believed that an anti-marriage spirit had literally taken over his once submissive wife. Amai was always spoiling for a divorce. Amai was doing everything that could have warranted her expulsion from the homestead.

She would always sing a traditional song, '*Kana ndoda kuramba murume ndoshereketa,*' or the *Katekwe* version of the traditional '*Warambiwa sara wega mugota, ndozvawaida kusara wega mugota,*' or '*Huya utore kadhora kako, kadhora kako ndinako pano.*' She would sometimes come home in the dead of the night, stone drunk and in the company of different men.

She had the guts to tell Baba off whenever he dared to question her wayward behaviour. She would in no uncertain terms challenge Baba in the face to free her by giving her a *gupuro*. A divorce token usually came in the form of the smallest denominations of a five or ten cent coin. Baba could not pluck up enough courage to offer the stubborn and defiant Amai that divorce token, but resolved to suffer in silence for the sake of the marriage of convenience.

I strongly suspected Amai of having doctored Baba with a heavy dosage of love potion. At one time, a determined Amai had shamelessly tossed a divorce token at Baba in our presence, challenging him to scoop it, but Baba simply ambled away in a walk of shame shedding tears of both shame and agony.

He had been reduced to a laughing stock.

I had never seen Baba weeping before. Maybe if he had wept before, he had done it in the dark like what all weak men do. Baba's spirit had been broken.

He could have committed suicide by hanging himself had it not been for Mukuwasha Furidhomu's timely intervention.

CHAPTER 33

KUNDISO

So convinced that a roving destructive anti-marriage spirit was on the prowl in our home, was Baba that he would spend most of his time visiting some white garment prophets who would prescribe different solutions to the problem that was bedeviling his marriage.

A marriage that Amai had vowed to put asunder, a marriage of convenience whose value Amai no longer cherished if at all there was any value to talk about in the first place.

The Holy Spirit would reveal to Baba the source of that spirit of destruction, Amai's late octogenarian aunt who had gone through the agony of six divorces in her miserable lifetime two generations back.

Those nasty divorces had left her energy sapped as she had born children by the gross, all in the hope of impressing all her husbands.

She kept on trying to piece together her marriages whenever cracks started to show, but she failed dismally and died stinking with poverty, malnourished, breasts shriveled from suckling before going down fighting a chronic disease of cervical cancer. Back then, the disease, which usually afflicted whites, was known in *Shona* as *nhuta*. It was associated with witchcraft. It was that anti-marriage spirit that had literally taken over and enveloped Amai who was behaving as if she were possessed.

Her actions were no longer consistent with those of a married woman. A woman who was once the envy of many in the neighbourhood. A woman who was once an embodiment of traditional values.

A woman who was once an oasis of peace building and reconciliation. She had reconstructed several bridges during her mediating roles. She had managed to bring warring spouses at a table to discuss peace. Amai had managed to dole out several peace pipes for everlasting smokes.

A countless number of households owed their existence to her diligence and peace broking prowess. She had managed to save several marriages from crumpling under the weight of anti-marriage spirits that would have been stalking some couples who would have been caught unaware.

But alas, she was no longer a paragon of honesty, faithfulness and integrity. She was no longer an epitome of peace, but an enigma, a riddle, a puzzle to the society she once towered over with her peace building techniques.

She was no longer the woman of virtue she once was. The reason being, a generational anti-marriage spirit was haunting her, desperate to drive her out of her matrimony and onto the streets.

Baba would be made to pray whilst biting a cake of soap, which he would later use to wash away that spirit with at *pamharadzano dzenzira*.

There in the middle of the night and middle of the bush, Baba would be expected to wash his body with rice, chicken fat and blood as well as milk, after which he would be required to turn the plastic dish with his heel.

He was expected to trudge and sneak home in the nude without turning back. Strolling home nichodemusly in the nude where he could have bumped into a son-in-law, a daughter-in-law, a grown up son, a grown up daughter and teenage niece, was a desperate measure. After all, a desperate situation calls for a desperate measure.

He had suffered enough ridicule at the hands of Amai who on countless occasions had dressed him down in the presence of all and sundry. To him, he no longer had any shred of *hunhu, ubuthu*, dignity to protect or preserve.

He had been literally stripped naked before, not once, not twice, not thrice, but at times without number.

He would collect the keeled over dish very early in the morning before anybody would have awoken up. He would immediately leave home to comb for jobs in the nearby Fern Valley neighbourhood.

Were the prophets indirectly advising Baba in their wisdom to be an early riser so as to catch the fattest worm? I wondered. Bhudhi Masango wondered, Bhudhi Maikoro also wondered, Mukuwasha Furidhomu wondered, so did Bhudhi Ranziroti.

All and sundry also joined in being wondering wonderers. We were all taking plunges and paddling in puddles of wonderland. We all wondered.

In a fraught and positive bid to stem the tide of raging flames of poverty, Amai and Sisi Garandichauya resolved to join other women who were involved in chicken slaughtering, plucking and dressing.

As an incentive, the women would be allowed to take home chicken feet, wings, heads, gizards and intestines. That enabled our family to enjoy descent meals.

Sisi Garandichauya's husband Mukuwasha Furidhomu who had been relieved off his job as a garden boy in the then Salisbury's had come to join the family since his parents had disowned him for marrying into a well-to-do-family.

Sons-in-laws of yesteryears were groomed to be *vakuwasha chaiwo*. They would never shake hands with their mother-in-laws. It was taboo, unexpected and unacceptable.

That was the very culture that was adopted by the Johane Masowe eChishanu in a bid to stem the tide of fornication and adultery. By the same measure, daughter-in-laws and father-in-laws were not allowed to shake hands.

Back then, boys and men used to show their intentions to would be lovers by way of scratching the palms of those they secretly admired during hand shaking. But then in Mount Darwin where my umbilical was entombed many years ago, men would not shake hands with women the reason being that the majority of women and girls were 'fenced or protected fields' which could only be unlocked by their owners.

Men who would have strayed into other men's beds or trespassed into other men's fields would die unless the men set them free upon payment of compensation whose field they would have plundered.

Sometimes, the adulterous pair would remain entangled in that horizontal position until they were set free. The setting free of an amorous couple was known as *kuwombonora*.

Sons-in-laws of yesteryears would greet their mothers-in-laws whilst crouching. That crouching would be accompanied, complemented and complimented by the clapping of hands known in the Korekore custom as *nhondo or gusvu*.

The mother-in-laws would reciprocate. This they would do even at the heart and soul of a city, along the periphery of pavements. In the morning, sons-in-laws were expected or rather tradition demanded that they greet their in-laws by way of clapping hands very early in the morning, the ungodly hours.

The father-in-laws were expected to reciprocate that gesture by way of clapping hands too, *kuuchira manja*.

The emergence of son-in-law Baba Anzikariya on the scene was a blessing in disguise, as fights that had become synonymous or rather had become a DNA of our parents, literally saw the gloves being thrown out through the window. As poverty continued to knock on our door, making herself a permanent feature on our doorstep, Amai enterprising as she was, ventured into the growing of *mbanje*, which she would peddle along with wine. That was done in a nearby bushy area.

Joy seekers would converge at our homestead to imbibe the highly intoxicating brew. Baba and Amai would also consume the brew.

CHAPTER 34

THE TRAP

Among those revellers was a middle-aged married woman of loose morals who had fallen for my boyish looks. Then I was around nine or so years. I was later told that the woman Mai Vhairedhi, had used some charms to lure me to bed where she would sexually assault me. She would continuously sexually abuse me to quench her insatiable sexual libido.

Her shenanigans became known when she infected me with a venereal disease, a sexually transmitted infection then known as *siki or njovhera*. My tiny manhood was afflicted with rare scabies that threatened to decapitate it. I would scratch at every turn leaving my fingers blood stained. One day, Mai Vhairedhi stumbled upon my hideout where I would scratch my itchy sausage until my fingers dripped with blood.

As soon as she appeared, my anaconda coiled ready to strike. She went behind a small shrub where she intended to relieve herself. She deliberately showed her backside whilst urinating. I literally went on all fours towards her. Within a short space of time, I was hungrily tugging at her sagging boobs whilst at the same time trying to remove her pant. At that juncture, her husband who had been suspecting that her wife could have been cheating with a Ben Ten, suddenly rustled and emerged from a thick bush that was a spitting distance from where we were about to engage in another of our steamy duels.

Mai Vhairedhi was mesmerized by the new twist of events. Love struck or rather thunder struck, she remained transfixed to the spot which we had intended to turn into a love nest. Trembling uncontrollable, I let off her boobs as I battled to pull up my badly patched pair of shorts.

Baba Vhairedhi who was equally bamboozled by what he had seen, tried to strip a nearby bush of one of her branches with which he intended to whip us with. But alas, he had underestimated our intelligence.

We bolted in the direction of where some revellers were, wailing. Baba Vhairedhi gave chase brandishing the whip and frothing at the mouth as he seethed with anger.

Confusion reigned supreme as revellers were thrown into sixes and sevens, as Baba Vhairedhi bayed for our blood. Sanity was finally restored following the timely intervention by two elderly couples the Shumbas and Mandeyas.

The elderly pair of couples and my parents who were fighting in my corner distancing me from the *hide my sausage adult game*, were fermenting with anger. They strongly believed that Baba Vhairedhi was levelling some weird and trumped up adultery charges.

During the *dare*, kangaroo Court, it was resolved that I maintained a distance from Mai Vhairedhi who I was ordered to view like my own mother.

But this Mai Vhairedhi was different from my mother, never exhibited any wife traits, was morally bankrupt and would never be my mother. Baba Vhairedhi was ordered to treat me like his son.

'*Hamuzivi kurwadza kunoita kuhurirwa nemukadzi pachena nemunhu waunoziva,*' he had blurted out before storming out of the hastily assembled kangaroo Court.

Mai Vhairedhi later owned up to Amai after she confronted her. She revealed to Amai how she had infected me with an STI. Amai ordered her to foot for my medical bills. I was taken to Nazareth Hospital in Sakubva where I was treated and discharged.

After recovering from that bout, I started to visualize the good times that I had shared with Mai Vhairedhi. Her images kept flooding into my memory bank as if from floodgates.

The more she stayed away from me, the more my love grew towards her. I could fantasize myself being intimate with Mai Vhairedhi.I could visualize myself massaging Mai Vhairedhi's bulging tummy which I had boldly claimed responsibility despite the fact that she was legally married to Baba Vhairedhi.

I could fantasize myself holding Mai Vhairedhi's bouncing baby boy whose paternity I had audaciously claimed. The way I fantasized with Mai Vhairedhi was not normal for a boy of my age and innocence. I now suspect that she might have used some charms to lure me. Some African charms like *mubobobo, mukwarakwato* or *gondwa waturuka,* a form of blue tooth used by witches and wizards to sexually abuse their victims unknowingly in their sleep or even during the day in public places, on the bus, train, or shows.

A fortnight had elapsed since that confrontation. When Baba Vhairedhi almost caught us in the act, an act of shame. I still shudder to think how my parents would have reacted at our sight.

I shudder to think how the entire community would have reacted upon setting their eyes on us, the affectionate duo.

I still shudder to think what was going to be left of me had the gangly and muscular Baba Vhairedhi decided to descend on me with the speed of a bolt of lightning and the destructive power of a sledgehammer. I still fail to plumb how I would have picked myself up from that walk of shame. I still shudder to think what I would have done if Baba Vhairedhi had resolved to slap his wife with a divorce token and dumped Amai Vhairedhi at our homestead.

Would I have married her? Would my parents and relatives have approved such an abnormal relationship, an abomination of a relationship?

I still shudder, shudder, shudder, shudder and shall continue to shudder.

I was roaming in shudderland when Amai Vhairedhi suddenly appeared at our homestead with a heavily bandaged leg. She was walking with a heavy flaccid. She later confided in me to what had happened to her leg, shedding tears of agony whilst leaning on my little shoulder.

CHAPTER 35

WIFE BATTERING, THE MYTH

My childhood sweetheart, Mai Vhairedhi had revealed to me how she had been brutalised and savaged by Baba Vhairedhi who wanted to put a leash on her by curtailing her movements.

When I heard that, a rush of pain rushed through my body. I felt for my childhood sweetheart, Mai Vhairedhi. A sharp pain punctuated with infatuated love had raced through my little heart.

I felt a tinge of jealousy. I felt love bound to avenge the injury and pain inflicted on Amai Vhairedhi. I felt an urge to waylay and murder my rival suitor Baba Vhairedhi. To me, he had done the unthinkable, that of thumping up a gorgeous lady.

To me, ladies of stunning beauty ought to remain untouched, unharmed, wanted and loveable. To me, they were a version of the Touch Not the Anointed.

Boys back then were brought up in traditional set ups that perpetuated and viewed domestic violence as normal and expected in any relationship. Girls then were taught to be culturally, sexually, morally, socially and physically submissive.

They were taught never to lift their fingers against their husbands no matter how physically weaker their spouses might appear to be.

They were taught never to engage in tongue lashing contests with their spouses. It was unheard of. It was taboo.

Back then, girls were brought up in homes that glorified women bashing as gentle and expected.

You would hear men or husbands bragging among their age mates or contemporaries, '*Mukadzi haafaniri kugara from January to December asina kumborohwa. Murume anofanira kutsvagira mukadzi wake mhosva kuti awane kumurova.*'

Husbands genuinely believed that, any husband who loved their wives would take time to physically reign in their errant wives especially those of bed hopping type like Mai Vhairedhi.

Men then strongly believed that any husband who dearly loved his wife would occasionally give her a thumping of a lifetime.

Talk of a spare the belt, fist or slap and spoil the wife. And once a woman was spoilt be it for choice or otherwise, she was spoilt indeed and forever.

If a woman escapes beating from her husband in the early days or years of their marriage and got a hiding in the twilight of that union, it would be a bad omen. Such a woman would be on her way out of her marriage, traditionalists reckoned.

Their men traditionally beat up women as a spice that curried their union. Couples who always brawled were regarded as super couples.

Those couples, it was believed, would always miss each other whenever circumstances demanded that they separated temporarily.

I hated Baba Vhairedhi for having beaten the blue out of my childhood sweetheart, Mai Vhairedhi. Mai Vhairedhi was dazzling beautiful, her skin was as soft as a parrot's breast to the touch.

She had a cherubic and angelic face that dazzled beholders. Anybody who would have set their eyes on her would have run short of superlatives and adjectives.

I must confess Mai Vhairedhi was more enticing when naked than when she was attired in any outfit the world could provide her with.

I had seen her in her birthday suit maybe more times than her husband had done. I had feasted my eyes on her at our rendezvous, just behind a huge *muhacha* tree that towered Amai's kachasu brewery.

There I had observed that she had tattoos in the forms of coloured incisions, on her bums, thighs, just under her sagging boobs, above her navel and an assortment of beads that dangled around her waist that had the effect of leaving lustful men sexually drained.

What surprised me was the fact that Mai Vhairedhi seemed to enjoy the act, my performance, my effort. She had taught me how I was supposed to carry myself when engaged in the adultery world. I had mustered the art so swiftly and exhibited great skills, which she strived to hone and perfect every time we met at our hideout. She always praised me for my performances.

To spice up those praises, she would incentivise me by doling out some crystal sweets that had peanut butter embedded at the centre as well as some Choice Assorted biscuits. She seemed to enjoy my bedroom antics that she would moan and groan with pleasure.

Whether it was feigned or genuine pleasure, that was for her to know and for me to find out, which I unfortunately never walked the trouble to do. She always wheedled me around telling me that my performance was better than that of Baba Vhairedhi.

Two months back, she had a miscarriage whose paternity she claimed I was responsible. I held my head low on hearing such devastating news whilst grappling to fight tears from cascading down my cheeks, tears that had welled up in my red shot eyes.

I was convinced that young as I was, I was medically responsible for her pregnancy, which unfortunately had failed to reach maturity.

She controlled me like a *yoyo* or a parody doll, held me spellbound by her striking beauty, beauty that was equally stunning, mesmerizing, bemusing, captivating and tantalizing. I had never seen any black woman who could match her beauty.

That was how passionate and compassionate about Mai Vhairedhi I had become. I was more than infatuated with her heavy dosages of love. I was simply obsessed with her to the point of not seeing any of her evil machinations. I was blindly blinded by her gorgeous looks, looks that had deceived so many a lustful man.

CHAPTER 36

HOUSE OF HORROR

A knifelike scream that sliced through the unruffled milieu drowned the area taking both human beings and phantoms that patrolled the hood by surprise. That scream was no ordinary, but a distraught one that was coupled with pain and despair.

I stretched out of our threadbare blankets after my five elder brothers had done so. I stealthily followed their footsteps to where the distress call was frantically calling for assistance. The distress call led them to the men's court, where Amai and Baba were involved in a fistfight.

The fight or rather battle was a ding-dong affair. The pendulum swung dangerously from one end to the other.

The outcome was just, but as unpredictable as a cornered rebel. At one time Amai could be seen pummelling the living day lights out of Baba whom he would have overpowered during a wrestling duel.

There she would be thumping Baba's face with wild abandon whilst Sisi Garandichauya and her husband Mukuwasha Furidhomu could be heard pleading with her to exercise some moderation, but Amai could not have any of that. She had the ogre of a husband cornered and was out to turn the tables. In no time, the tables would be turned in Baba's favour. Baba would have Amai back peddling and pleading for foreign intervention, which would come in the form of Mukuwasha Furidhomu who chose to play the mediating role.

Baba who could not take any of those pleas, was determined to ascertain and perpetuate his dominance over Amai.

Upon realizing that Baba's determination could end in tragedy as he was choking Amai with a vice like grip, Mukuwasha Freedom whose name had been corrupted to Furidhomu, took the bull by its horns going against tradition. Tradition then dictated that in-laws were untouchables.

When Amai swiftly broke clear from the clutches of Baba's grip following Mukuwasha Furidhomu's intervention, she immediately launched some sporadic raids on Baba who was being restrained by Mukuwasha.

Even though I was young then, I could tell that Mukuwasha had dismally failed to sit it out on the fence. He had failed to observe neutrality as demanded by his role and had taken sides with Amai.

After Baba realised Mukuwasha's motives, in his drunken stupor, he vented his anger against Mukuwasha by delivering a barrage of punches that sent Mukuwasha sprawling to the ground.

My elder brothers and Sisi Garandichauya who had been watching the proceedings, quickly moved in to separate Baba who was then spoiling for a duel against Mukuwasha who had been taken aback by the twist of events. Later, we all trooped out to our respective bedrooms after the tempers had been cooled down. Amai who had escaped from the clutches of death, sought sanctuary in the girls' bedroom.

The following day, Baba failed to wake up from his bedroom as usual. Not because he was suffering from a terrible hangover, the reason being he had been gripped with a tornado of shame.

He could not afford to face the whole family worse still Mukuwasha whom he had descended upon with a hurricane of blows. He had to feign illness. He simply could not afford to walk the walk of shame with his head bowed low and down.

He blamed evil spirits and beer for his highs. He promised to take a sabbatical break from beer binges and possibly return to the pulpit where he was once called, but later on resolved to turn his back on the Messiah.

It took almost a fortnight for the situation to normalize. When the desert storm finally subsided, we were astounded to see Baba and Mukuwasha moving hand in hand in their drunken stupor coming from Chigomba in Dangamvura.

In most cases, they would be singing under their drunken wave *katekwe* songs from Mt Darwin. Sometimes they would show us a few fancy footwork on the dance floor. Baba would turn to his *mbira,* the African piano for solace, which he would strum with gusto and aplomb of a distinguished veteran. He would also blow his penny whistle as he reminisced and strutted his *ngororombe* playing skills. A fortnight later, a dark cloud enveloped our family. I was alone at home.

My elder siblings who attended Sheni Primary School in

Dangamvura had gone to school, which was about twenty kilometres away.

Amai and Sisi Garandichauya had gone to Fern Valley where they were engaged in a chicken plucking venture at Baas Van Voerren's residence. Baba, Mukuwasha and Bhudhi Masango who were out of employment had gone to the city to comb for employment.

It was around midday when I heard the rumbling of a police vehicle, a Land Rover model coughing, puffing and huffing over a hilly terrain that led to our adopted homestead. In no time, two white police officers alighted from the Jeep before it could be brought to a halt.

One of them held me by my nose whilst the other one squeezed my ears, which burnt with excruciating pain. The duo was heavily armed. They threatened to blow my head with their assault rifles if I chose not to cooperate with their investigations.

I was held spell bound by their bandoliers and shiny calf covers that shone brightly under the June colonial sun. The one who held me by the nose, whacked me across my face, sending me tumbling down a slope. I was saved from further sliding into an abyss that had been formed after my family had embarked in a brick-moulding project for the construction of Mukuwasha Furidhomu's bedroom. The other one followed me with a flurry of kicks that left me spewing blood. I had to feign death but urine and diarrhoea that cascaded and dripped down my swarthy legs sold me away.

In no time, a squadron of flies were circling and hovering over my body whilst the white officers who had been threatening to unleash a pack of dogs on me, held and wriggled their noses spitting in the process.

The police officers who could not stand the pong zoomed off leaving behind a trail of dust that left me engulfed in a Shekinah-like cloud. Before driving off, the officers had promised to come back for me. I picked myself up, dusted myself and headed straight to the men's court where I slumped in an old sofa that squeaked as if in both pain and protest. I nursed my wounds there. I cleaned my wounds using a concoction of methylated spirit, salt mixed with soot which I had plucked from our traditional kitchen where it dangled with reckless abandon.

When Amai and Sisi Garandichauya finally arrived, they found me tucked in between blankets. I was feeling a bit under the weather due to the injuries that I had picked during that short encounter with the brutal duo of the British South African Police. I revealed what had happened. Amai and Sisi Giroriya knew what the mabhurakwachas were after. They were after marijuana that Amai used to sell.

CHAPTER 37

THE TIP-OFF

Somebody from our community might have sold Amai out. We all suspected Amai Andimu our neighbour who she had clashed with a few days back after she had brought a live python that had swallowed four of her chickens to Baba suggesting that they could make money by selling it off to the Umtali Museum.

Amai who had long suspected that Baba and Amai Andimu could have been involved in an adulterous affair, blew her top and threatened to give Amai Andimu a thorough bashing of her life.

Amai had gone to label Amai Andimu a witch who had plans to initiate Baba so that they would form a formidable partnership on two fronts.

Amai having smelt a fat rat had taken Sisi Garandichauya and me to where she had kept her contraband, which we moved to a new and safer site.

But then, a rat is a rat, fat or otherwise. After relocating to a new base, we made sure our tracks were well covered. Maybe we thought we had our tracks covered well. A week later, true to their promise the mabhurakwachas came back for me. Once again, I was alone at home when they pounced unsuspectedly. This time they left their marked vehicle at a distance and stealthily came crawling. One of them a black detective who was dressed like a farm supervisor approached me disguised as a client.

He lied to me that he wanted to buy the illegal drug in large quantities and so wanted to be shown around the *warehouse* so as to be sure of a constant supply of the drugs.

With poverty having knocked our door and sending parental love through the window in the process, I thought we had finally struck it rich. I showed him around the new warehouse without smelling any rat.

I told him all he needed to know like a good marketing officer. I revealed to him some revelations that I was not supposed to reveal. When we returned home, he revealed to me how I had given away the family secret, the warehouse, the source of income, the source of dirty money.

The plain-clothes detective force-marched me to where their unmarked vehicle was. I was ordered to accompany the law enforcement agents to where Amai was. The detective identified himself to Amai's employer Baas Van Voerren who gave him the greenlight to arrest Amai.

Baas Van Voerren could not have stood in the way of the police as that could have seen him being charged with trying to obstruct the course of justice. *What justice? Whose justice? Which justice?*

Amai was whisked away by Det Cst Tanyanyiwa who shepherded her to the police vehicle that was parked a distance away. I was left in the care of Sisi Garandichauya. As the police Jeep carried her way out of Baas Van Voerren's yard, it finally dawned on me that I had sold Amai out unknowingly. Pangs of guiltiness gripped me.

Tears of guilt welled up my eyes. Tears of pain and tears of realisation cascaded down my cheeks, down, down my mucus-smeared face, the face of poverty.

I wailed uncontrollably when it finally sunk that Amai had been arrested for peddling mbanje and might probably do time for that offence. Should that happen, everybody would blame me for being too revealing, for failing to read the inquisitiveness of Det Cst Tanyanyiwa.

That I thought all to myself. The more I thought of the consequences of the case, the more I shed tears of despair for Amai. The more I thought of the gravity of the case, the more tears trickled down like a deluge of poverty.

Sisi Garandichauya joined in the race of tear shedding. Together we shed tears of hopelessness. Tears of torture. Tears of terror. Tears of horror.

As siblings, we were horrified at the prospect of losing Amai to the prison walls. We had heard a lot of stories concerning prison life. Life there was not a bed of roses. Life there was not a stroll in the park. Life there was not an amble down the aisle.

Baas Van Voerren, released Sisi Garandichauya whom she ordered to take me home. Many questions awaited me. A lot of blame and finger pointing awaited me. Amai's predicament was to be blamed squarely on me;

I was to stand accused of failing to reign in my loose tongue. I was to be taken to task over the incarceration of Amai, the breadwinner.

And how prophetic and true to my words I was. Everybody blamed me for having played a pivotal role or worse still for having masterminded the incarceration of Amai. As accusations and counter accusations flew thick and fast, I lost my marbles and dared any of my siblings who accused me of contributing to the arrest of Amai, to an open fight. I told whoever cared to listen that I had given away the family's breadwinner because I had never been schooled in secret keeping.

I told those present that I did not own a suitcase in which I was supposed to keep that secret in secrecy.

CHAPTER 38

DIARY FROM THE GHETTO

I had been enjoying the act far from the madding crowd. It was fast becoming a routine or rather I had been slowly drifting into an addiction of some sort. The place appeared leafy, cool and seemed to be in agreement with Mother Nature.

Tranquillity and serenity always reigned supreme. It was only the sound of humming birds, baritoning loudly for their birdlie supper that always brought me back to reality.

I had made that place, far from the hustle and bustle of ghetto life, my place. Yes, I was slowly laying claim to that place that was far away from prying and preying eyes of the ghetto, a ghetto that had a long nose.

A long nose that always poked into affairs that did not concern it leaving behind a trail of mucus that badly needed to be wiped away.

I was there lying prostrate on a bed of luscious green grass that blended well with my shredded clothes.

You would be forgiven for thinking that I was a member of the Jacknation, *Jekenisheni,* Apostolic Sect, the one they refer to as *rumurenzi, magopito* or simply splinters. I was lying a spitting distance away from an adulterous couple that was enjoying carnal knowledge of each other. Yes, they were busy munching away the forbidden fruit like hungry rabbits, far from the community glare. I could hear the woman moaning and groaning with pleasure.

I could see a myriad of dazzling beads, which adorned her waist. Her milk oozers were dangling and popping out of a pair of brazier that was held together by some strings.

Her pant and petticoat that were torn and tattered as if they had been under termite siege, lay strewn far from where she had made her makeshift bed.

The man, who also appeared to be deeply engrossed in the act, seemed relaxed as he serenaded with the groans and moans of the amorous act. During that act, I had realised that the woman was Amai Charisi who was married to a security guard.

The man who had illegally taken over the *fatherly role* from Baba Charisi was Baba Farai, a salesman from the DMB. The neighbourhood was awash with news of Amai Charisi's adulterous antics.

The previous week, three boys from the hood had caught her with a new pastor from her church with her torn pants down.

She had been made to lay her head on the pastor's Bible who upon realizing that some naughty boys had stumbled upon them from the community, had suddenly said, 'I command the spirit of bad luck to come out of her womb.'

The Naughty Trio then had laughed their lungs out before disappearing into the inviting arms of the *ghoulish* ghetto.

A fortnight back, she was again busted in a compromising position by a group of *Ruwadzano* women from her church in the company of Madzibaba Crynage, a popular prophet from the Johane Masowe sect who plied his fetish trade in the hood.

Madzibaba Crynage was strongly believed to have been the one who had cast out her spirit of bareness. Because of the spiritual powers vested in the *man of God*, two of her sons, Charisi and Joromiya bore resemblance to the man of God.

After all, Madzibaba Crynage had gained notoriety in the hood for his questionable modus operandi of spiritual healing. He was in the habit of using his manhood during cleansing ceremonies that involved women.

He usually *prophesied* about evil spirits being embedded in the ovaries, *mamhepo emuchibereko*. The only solution that he offered would be to use his manhood as a mantle for cleansing. A lot of married women who were desperate to save their marriages from crumpling, at any cost, had succumbed to Madzibaba Crynage's bizarre ways of spiritual healing.

Madzibaba Crynage was also in the habit of *removing incisions* on naked women, *kukwesha nyora,* using coarse salt, fresh milk and lemons.

Those incisions which he always prophesied to be behind bad luck would be *removed spiritually* in a makeshift grass thatched changing house that he had constructed far from the crowd, prying eyes and inquisitive minds.

As a result of his dubious operations, a lot of children in the hood bore resemblance of him as well as some prophetic traits. Quite a number would times without number slip into trances just like their *father.*

That was Madzibaba Crynage for you, a prophet held in high esteem by women whose marriages he had salvaged from the wreck. Men, whose wives would have visited him for spiritual guidance, would not pluck up enough courage to challenge his strange ways of spiritual healing.

The entire community feared his *spiritual powers.* The few who had dared him ended up dead and buried. He was a member of the much feared Johane Masowe *Yenguwo Tsvuku* feared for their penchant for *spiritual duels* which the prophets would constantly engage in.

Paternity, paternity, paternity and this *kushandirwa* business was something I tell you. There was this other apostolic church founded by a woman, Mutumwa Rachero believed to have been very powerful spiritually.

This sect tucked on the outskirts of Umtali, whose female congregants were always draped in white garbs with matching head covering cloths, had devised means to cure bareness among women whose husbands had low sperm counts. Women whose conditions were bordered on bareness were required to visit the church's shrine without their husbands. There they would then be ushered into single rooms and instructed to strip naked in readiness for sexual encounters with *ngirozi*, angels, which were later exposed as *mabhuru.*

The angels or *mabhuru* would descend or rather fly into those rooms with their faces covered to conceal their identities. The angels would make love to the women who would be instructed to continue with their visits until they would have conceived.

That way several marriages, which would have gone asunder, were saved. That way, the founder of the sect maintained her spiritual powers.

That way the *miracle babies* which were stage managed, but genuinely believed to be God given in the eyes of congregants and those blessed with fruits of the womb, propped *mutumwa's* credentials and spiritual prowess.

The shenanigans of this church came to light when a suspicious husband who had refused to be hoodwinked, clandestinely followed his wife to the shrine. When his wife entered into her cubicle in readiness for the angelic services, the husband waited in wait.

All of a sudden, a gangly angel flew into the booth for another healing session. The husband flew into a rage, surged into the cubicle and descended on the angel with a flurry of blows that sent him sprawling to the ground. Before the dazzled angel could come to terms with events of that morning, the enraged and frothing husband went for the mask, unmasking the angel in the process. The unmasked angel having realized that the game was up, took to flight ascending into a cloud of dust.

That was how the angels were exposed and unmasked. The husband who was still seething with anger, picked his stark naked and baffled wife, helped her to dress up before laying siege on the church shrine.

That was how hell broke loose at the shrine. Paternity, paternity, paternity is as controversial a subject as they come.

This was the reason why the true paternity of Amai Charisi's other two sons Jobho and Jairos could be traced and linked to Amukaka, the milk salesman and the butcher boy respectively.

The local grinder, who always made sure that the family would not go hungry, laid claim on the fifth son Jericho.

Rumours that were circulating in the community of Sakubva in general and Matida Flats in particular where she stayed, were that she had had her uterus surgically removed after succumbing to a plethora of sexually transmitted diseases.

Had her uterus not been removed, she would have borne the pastor and shopkeeper some children for she believed in bearing children by the gross.

Whenever word filtered into the ears of the husband, Baba Charisi the doctored one, that she had been caught in the act again, he would seethe and foam at the mouth with anger threatening to send her packing to her parents' home in Dora Dombo.

But once she arrived, he would change goal posts and blame the community for trying to drive a wedge between him and his beautiful wife. That would give credence to the rumour that Baba Charisi must have been fed with an over doze of *mupfuhwira*. In a bid to douse the flames of the rumours from consuming their relationship, the couple would move house to another section of the sprawling suburb, a suburb in which all sorts of social ills and vices were abound.

A neighbourhood that feeds and survives on rumours. A neighbourhood that thrives on the commission of crimes some of which have defied criminology. A neighbourhood in which Angels sometimes fear to tread on.

Amai Charisi must have been gifted in the game that is usually venued between the sheets, if the milkman's face that would contort and grimace with pleasure was anything to go by. As I watched live, their pornographic images, young, but adulterated as I was, I wished I could also sample her.

My desire to have a go at her were aroused and heightened after I had watched her in the nude as she took her time to dress. Of course, she had to take her time during dressing because should she choose to be swift, she would be left holding on to *mamvemve*.

After breaking a fall as she tried to slip her leg through her badly holed pant, I heard her asking for a new pair of undergarments from the milkman.

'*Amukaka munobhohwa imi, chamunogona kubvisa nekudhambisa mabhurugwa akatengwa nemurume wangu, but imi hamudi kutenga.*'

The milkman could be heard responding in a lowered tone laced with embarrassment, '*Ndapota usagumbuke kana kukwidza zvako izwi. Ziva kuti nyika ine nzeve nemaziso. Ndanzwa Chipo, ndichazama kukutengera kana mwedzi wapera,*' as he shied away his badly torn underwear that revealed his backside.

CHAPTER 39

THE ILLICIT AFFAIR

Mai Charisi retorted angrily, '*Amukaka wenyu mwedzi hauperi apa futi ndaneta nezvimukaka zvenyu ini. Munhu wepi akaomera kudaro. Dai kuri kurambwa nemurume wangu ndorambirwa tumikaka itwotwo. Kuzodawo kundipa mwana kani. Pakukuitira mwana ndakairasa. Iwe ungazogone kunditengera bhurugwa remukati uchitadza kutenga rako kana remukadzi wako, dai chisi chiro.*'

Milk then, both fresh and sour, was a delicacy, a status symbol. The heeled ones or those from middle class could buy some milk coupons that would enable them to receive Dairy Marketing Board milk bottles at their doorsteps on a daily basis. Nobody then had the audacity to steal milk from doorsteps even in the high-density suburbs.

After being given a poignant piece of sarcastic and brutal frankness by Amai Charisi, Amukaka walked away down the hill in a walk of shame leaving Amai Charisi to tie her *zambia*.

She too rolled away in a roll of shame down the hill skirting the United Methodist Church's Hilltop Assembly. I picked myself up and tailed her from a distance. I did not want to give myself away for I had something up my sleeve. Amai Charisi passed through a butchery at *paChigomba* where she collected some bones, which she would mix with some vegetables. Just like other struggling women from the hood, all she wanted was to have the tasty taste of meat in the relish.

In return, for that she had borne the butcher boy a son. When I got home in the National Housing Board section of Sakubva, Amainini Rusiya had not yet returned from *Musika weHuku* where she was still slugging it out with her compatriots.

Just like my father, her husband had also walked out on her and was co-habiting with a single mother who was employed at Sunlo. Houses in the NHB were then meant for bachelors.

Women and children were not supposed to be seen living in those houses. We were outlawed to leave in those houses. Women and children were meant to stay in kraals in the tribal trust lands under a kraal head who would sometimes stray into his subjects' unprotected kraals to devour some hapless cows.

Some kraal heads would prey on women whose husbands barred them from visiting the locations. To minimize infidelity by women who would have been fallow for months on end, some husbands would not allow their wives to wash their privates the moment they stepped onto the bus back to their urban bases.

Houses in the Block Section, McGreggors, Muchena, Maonde, OTS, Chimoio Flats, Matida Hostels, Mundembe, Old Location and Chisamba Singles now known as *muJapan* were also meant for singles.

To enforce that law, the Rhodesian police would regularly carry out some routine inspections coupled with some pre-dawn and pre-dusk raids into those areas. During raids, women and children would take refuge in some nearby bushes that provided some sanctuaries.

The refugees in a land of plenty, would only sneak into their homes in the dead of the night, after 10 pm. Playing hide and seek with authorities was not black township dwellers' only problem. They had to grapple with food, which was scarce. Some meals had to be scrapped off the food menu or food chart. In the morning, most children would be fed with porridge that would have been flavoured with baobab fruits

Pinches of bicarbonate soda would sometimes be added to the porridge to give it an appealing and appetising golden colour.

Money has always been a scarce commodity. It was worse in the townships where most households were run on shoestring budgets. But then, most shoes did not have shoe laces. I wonder whose shoe strings were used then.

Siblings would wash their hands in the same dirty water without anyone succumbing to dysentery or cholera. Whenever there was a cholera outbreak especially in the tribal trust lands, some of the afflicted would have to confess to witchcraft to survive. Failure to do so would result in death. Most of those in the Tribal trust lands viewed cholera as a disease that would clean up communities of witches. Cholera then behaved like witch hunters of the calibre of *Tsikamutandas* or *Gauranis*.

In some of those communities, there were known magicians who possessed powers to whip witches into line using some doctored whips. Others would drive some doctored nails into witches' heads.

A witch who would have a nail driven into their heads during their nocturnal escapades would complain of a migraine headache before passing on. That was how populations were kept in check then.

Having washed hands in the same dirty water, children would hungrily eat from the same plate, fought over bones that were bare of meat and swum in the same soup. Bedtime presented another headache for parents. Beds had to be raised using bricks to accommodate children born by the unsophisticated. Those children would engage in fierce battles over some tattered and urine drenched blankets.

Those who were in the habit of bed wetting would be asked to dry their blankets out for all and sundry to see. Sometimes sisters and brothers would share blankets under raised beds. Boys would sometimes be loaned out or shipped out to male relatives whose wives would have heeded the Smith regime's call to stay in the reserves or tribal trust lands as the rural areas were then called.

CHAPTER 40

SQUABBLING OVER SQUABBLES

Squabbles over who should spread or make some make shift beds would always break out among siblings. There were some children who didn't want to make beds or to remove blankets that would have covered them the previous night.

Usually the early risers would get away with it. It was the late birds who would have to remove those blankets, which might be dripping with urine. And they risked being nicknamed *nyaweti*.

Fights over who should get bread crust were the order of the day. Siblings then would fight over *kuruvota* which was a syrup made from water and sugar, a substitute for tea.

In a desperate bid to make ends meet following the departure of Babamunini Ferekisi, Amainini Rusiya resorted to prostitution. She hooked up with a live-in boyfriend Mairosi who worked as a municipal police officer, *mugombojena*, white legged or *mudengu munei?* The nosy ones as they were derogatorily referred to as.

The municipal police officers would not let a woman carrying a sisal bowl pass by without asking about the contents of that bowl. These bowls were associated with vegetable and fruit vendors who used them as carrier bowls.

Mairosi's wife and kids stayed in the tribal trust lands of Zviyambe, Hwedza where she laboured to give their homestead a homely appearance.

There she took care of the family's six cattle and ten goats. There she would wait to be given alms by Mairosi, alms that would have been left by Amainini Rusiya.

Amainini Rusiya had developed notoriety for stripping men she would have dated, off their fortunes. Those she had dated were all left counting the costs of having invited her into their lives.

She would squeeze them out of their hard-earned wages, their pittances. Mairosi's wife would wait to be ploughed by Mairosi's tired ploughshare, a share that would have ploughed some foreign furrows.

She would wait for her annual work-over by Mairosi when he came home laden with groceries for the Christmas holiday. Mairosi would not allow her to visit him in the *rokesheni*.

Real African women stayed in the villages, the Tribal trust lands where they would labour to give their homesteads a homely appearance hence the adage *musha mukadzi*.

In order to milk as much money from Mairosi's meagre salaries, Amainini Rusiya would instruct me to address him as Baba. Baba my foot!

I had sad memories of a father, Baba.

CHAPTER 41

THE AMBUSH

After Amainini Rusiya realised that Mairosi's resources were dwindling, she dumped him for Robati.

The estranged Mairosi who had been reduced to a pauper, moved in with Judesi who was still single, young and vivacious. She earned her keeps at Sunlo. Amainini Rusiya co-habited with Robati, a beerhall cashier from Murapa Tavern.

I had to address Robati as Baba. When Soromoni, a butcher boy from Munowenyu, moved in with Amainini Rusiya, I was supposed to address him as Baba as well, but I refused to play ball.

In a conceited effort to force me to comply, Soromoni had to use minimum force, that further strained our relationship, and I vowed to get even with that monster who had kept me under siege.

I was well acquainted with Soromoni's workplace just like the back of my hand. One day, I mooted a sinister idea that I shared with Charisi. I knew that Soromoni would ride home, the place I had adopted as my home since my mother left me under Amainini Rusiya's care.

I was no longer attending school having dropped out in Standard 3 at Mutanda Primary School after realising how thin an academic talent I was.

Charisi, who was my contemporary and age-mate, was still a pupil at Zamba Primary School deep at the heart of Sakubva, was already in Standard 5.

I was enrolled late at school because I did not have a birth certificate. The other reason that was being proffered by Amainini Rusiya for not sending me to school at age seven was that I had previously struggled to touch my left ear using my right hand via my head.

That was a test then used by some illiterate black parents who would have forgotten the actual ages of their children. That archaic and degradable test disadvantaged children who had tiny frames like me. By the time I passed that traditional test, I had already turned thirteen.

Besides, Amainini Rusiya wanted to use me as an errand boy to her myriad of boyfriends. Whenever she wanted to send me on an urgent errand, she would spit on the ground before instructing me to return before her spit would have dried up.

I would run off at a breakneck speed to wherever I would have been sent. Times without number, I would return with feedbacks before her spit would have dried up. That accomplishment had many incentives. She would spoil me with candy cakes and Happy Chap chocolate coned ice cream. As time sauntered to 10pm the exact time Soromoni was supposed to knock off, Charisi and I armed ourselves with some whips and a wire which we tied across the very path Soromoni was supposed to ride through on his way to his adopted home, where I lived.

After tying the wire across the path, we waited for our would-be victim. After a few minutes, we heard the jovial Soromoni cycling and whistling home. Soon, he ran into the wire trap that sent him flying into the air before landing with a thunderous thud.

Before he could recollect, we had descended on him lashing and striking him with the whips. We also poured ground chillies into his eyes.

We quickly slipped into the darkness that gladly swallowed us when some residents were swiftly beginning to respond to Soromoni's distress calls for help.

By the time assistance came to Soromoni, we had already made good our escape enveloped by the darkness. By the time Soromoni limped home, his clothes tattered, torn to smithereens and blood stained, I was already feigning to be sleeping soundly under the raised bed. I had settled my scores with Soromoni. Amainini Rusiya warmed some water, which she mixed with soot to prepare a medicinal concoction with which she used to dress Soromoni's fresh and blood oozing wounds.

He would wince with pain as Amainini Rusiya worked on the wounds. That night, I slept peacefully as the night was devoid of Amainini Rusiya's stage managed moans and groans of passion. That night, the rickety and metallic three quarter bed that Amainini Rusiya shared with Soromoni, never creaked, squeaked or coughed as if in protest. That night, I slept soundly like an infant. I had accomplished my mission of dispensing a bitter tasting medicine to Soromoni.

Soromoni never suspected that the misfortune that had befallen him could have been my work. Soromoni only came to know about the real events of the cadaverous night after Charisi and I had crossed swords following disagreements over the sharing of spoils from a wallet that I had picked up in the neighbourhood.

CHAPTER 42

SMOKING THE PEACE PIPE

Charisi, who I had given a lesser amount, decided to turn coat and spilled the beans to Soromoni. That very night, Soromoni packed his clothes and returned to his council rented apartment in the adjacent Matida Hostels plunging Amainini's household into abject poverty.

All she was left with were tongues of rays of the sun that were constantly cast in the direction of our lodgings. She was left to rue the day she had accepted me in. Only sweet memories of the good times that Soromoni and her had had, remained imbedded in her mind.

Angered by what I had done, a move that had resulted in Soromoni moving out, Amainini Rusiya resolved to throw me out of the house for a week in which I was taken in by Amai Roisi, one of her best friends who stayed in the Muchena section.

After being let off the hook, I set about scheming to play a fast one on my erstwhile friend Charisi who had led to my temporary banishment from home. I pretended to have forgiven Charisi for the role he had played in my debacle.

At first, Charisi was suspicious of my reconciliation manoeuvres, but with the passage of time, he was carried away with the reconciliation gambits I appeared to have extended. Blindly, he shared the peace pipe with me.

A week after the farce that had seen me being temporarily thrown out of the house by Amainini Rusiya, I resolved to even scores with Charisi. I wanted to teach him a lesson of a lifetime.

I approached his mother one mid-morning. She was alone at home. When I arrived, she was tucked in between the sheets trying to drift into an early siesta. I had panted out through a flight of stairs of Matida Hostels to her room. I knocked on her door.

After getting no response, I increased the intensity of my knock. Amai Charisi suddenly appeared from the doorway skimpily attired in a revealing morning gown, stretching her limbs in the process.

She must have been dazzled to see me that time of the day. I had never darkened her door during that time of the day. I usually visited her place well in the afternoon after Charisi would have returned from school. She knew that something was amiss. She invited me into her room and offered me a seat on a rickety bench that was mourning for some facelift. She slipped back into bed. Her tired and dilapidated bed that had been through a lot of pummelling that had resulted in a gross of children, wailed as if in pain.

Two of its legs had long been amputated and replaced with some artificial limbs, eight common bricks. I chose not to seat on the bench and instead joined her on her matrimonial bed uninvited.

She was taken aback by my actions as shown by her mouth, which had dropped ajar to her jaws. Before she could admonish me against my actions, I slipped into her blankets. I could feel her warmth and feminine attraction.

Before long, I was tugging, fumbling, caressing and fondling her tired breasts that hung loosely from her chest. They appeared flat and shaggy as if they had gone through a tagging contest.

To make them appear succulent and plump, Amai Charisi and other women from the hood used some cone shaped cardboard boxes as bra cups. That spruced up their bust. Having collected from her shock, she asked me what I was up to.

I told her point blank that I had come to sample her the way Amukaka had done that day behind that *madhorosiya* bush near the imposing United Methodist Church Hilltop Assembly.

CHAPTER 43

THE BLACKMAILER

She knew that her game was up as she was against a cunning young blackmailer from the location. She knew the consequences of refusing to play ball. I would tip-off Baba Charisi.

I would also impress upon him the need to go through a traditional paternity test. She was caught between a hard rock and a deep red sea. Should she deny me my *conjugal rights*, she risked being sent packing to her rural home and should she comply and infect me with a sexual transmitted infection, the world would be awash with news of our improper association. That would ruin her chequered reputation, a reputation that left a lot to be desired. Either way she was doomed.

I needed her services. I needed her to gratify the sexual libido that had been aroused at a tender age. She had no choice, but to play ball. She slipped out of the tattered blankets, went over to lock the door before stripping naked in front of me.

I was held spellbound by a plethora of multi-coloured beads that adorned her enticing waist. They made her a spectacle worth spectating and salivating at. Indeed, she was a belle in her own way. No wonder why *Amukaka* could not have enough of her.

Young as I was, I had seen a number of naked women before and I must admit that the Crafter and Creator of the Universe, the Almighty, ingenuinely crafted Amai Charisi. Her anatomy had an immediate effect on my dick, boyhood.

Back in the day, Dick was a popular name. Then it meant what it was intended to mean, but now it has been corrupted to mean something else, something hidden, something from the underworld, an important private part of all males.

Having been aroused by what I had seen, I began to work on her body. She appeared to be better than my former *wife* Amai Vhairedhi who had ushered me into the adulated adult world.

Amai Charisi was shocked by my experience. Amai Vhairedhi had corrupted me from a tender age. I got down to play with my *usanga* exploring her body. With my petite teenage hands, I caressed every part of her body worth caressing. She really enjoyed the corporeal massage. In no time, she was moaning and groaning with pleasure, more than what I had heard her doing the day I saw her being bonked by *Amukaka* the milkman. As I listened to her harp of pleasure, I could not help, but admire my sublime skills from the underworld, the forbidden fruit.

CHAPTER 44

HARP OF PASSION

I was perplexed by her fancy footwork as she gyrated to the rhythm of the harp of passion. She was an expert in the *forbidden dance*. It was then that I realised that Amai Vhairedhi had not feigned her moans and groans. They were genuine, real, not a fantasy, fallacy or stage-managed.

A porn star had been born. I only got to leave her room around 3pm after she had implored me to release her so that she could go and meet Amukaka at their rendezvous.

At first, I could not take that as an excuse. I was determined to have her to myself after I had sampled her. I was not prepared to share her with anybody else, even Baba Charisi. She had swept me off my feet.

As I left her room after she had promised to dish me another steamy roller coaster the following day, I could vividly hear a monster of a song from the 70s rocking into my ears

I wanted to have a monopoly over Amai Charisi. I wanted to have access to her as and when I wanted. I vowed to supply her with all her needs as I battled to elbow some of her boyfriends. I was thunder struck with hate and drugged with jealousy. Indeed, I had found love in Amai Charisi. That night I could not bat an eyelid as I continued to drift into fantasyland. The following day, I was at Amai Charisi's place earlier than the previous day.

I found her in bed with Baba Charisi who was enjoying his conjugal rights having just returned from a night shift slot. She wanted to dismiss me like a nobody, a teenager who was naïve, but I stood my ground.

She had to persuade me to leave promising me another unforgettable session in the afternoon. A week after my sexual encounter with Amai Charisi, Amainini Rusiya began to notice some changes in my behaviour. I had stopped hanging around with my age mates.

I would frequent Amai Charisi's room as well as Sekuru Rafurodhi's lodgings who had successfully treated me of a sexually transmitted infection that I had contracted from my newly found lover, my sugar mama Amai Charisi.

I had also sought to increase my performance through a concoction of some traditional aphrodisiacs like *Mudanhatsindi*. I also began to steal from Amainini Rusiya. I would pilfer some household goods like salt, sugar, mealie-meal, cooking oil, flour and skimmed milk. I would refer to Charisi as *my son*. After all, I was bedding his mother. I felt he ought to respect me as I was putting food on the family's table. I had turned into Amai Charisi's soulmate, a genuine soul provider.

I had vowed to turn the tables against Amai Charisi's boyfriends. When Amainini Rusiya discovered that I had been siphoning her household items, she sought to catch me red handed. Amai Charisi and I were virtually inseparable. I would accompany her everywhere even to the communal bathroom where I would be disguised as a Tom Boy. There I would feast my eyes on a myriad of women from the hood.

There I would hear women discussing their husbands' strengths and weaknesses in the inner room. There I had heard women bosting or rubbishing their husbands' menhoods.

There I had heard, unedited and seen women comparing and contrasting their God given assets, the boobs, bums, shapely legs and hairy chests. There I had seen some flat chests and bums. There I had seen a lot of tattered and torn undergarments. There I had seen some unshaven and clean shaven women.

No one could suspect that a peeping Tom was within their midst. There I had learnt to behave and talk like women, grown up women to be precise. In there I had to carry myself like a girl as I battled to keep my cover.

CHAPTER 45

THE RUMOUR MILL

As weeks wheeled off, the hood was awash with news of my improper association with Amai Charisi. Amai Charisi dismissed the rumour with the contempt it deserved.

'*Kana kuri kuzi ndine shavi rechihure ndipo pandingadananewo naTobhiyasi mwana wezuro achine mukaka pamhuno here? Zera raCharisi angandigutse here bonde racho? Zvimwe zvamunotaura anhu emuno muSakubva munombozvitorepi? Asikana musadaro ba, hamutsveruki here kutaura magumba anonyadzisa kudaro.*'

When Baba Charisi got wind of the rumours from the rumour mill that was tumbling fast and furious, he too dismissed them with disdain.

'*Amwe akadzi emuno muSakubva mwakude kuchaiwa ndini manje. Kana arume enyu asikamuchayi ini ndinomuchaya. Ngeyi mwechifamba mwechironza zvisina basa. Kushaya mabhuyo here? Kuti musina zvekuita zviya joinai makirabhu eakadzi pane kuswera kubhuya zvisina shwiro, zvisina nesoro,*' a pissed off Baba Chari was heard one day ranting in reaction to the rumours. When some overzealous women from the hood confronted me with the rumour, I gave them a piece of my mind, challenging them to a bedroom contest.

'*Asi muri kundidawo kani? Kana muchindidawo munotaura zvakanaka kwete kuswero tenderera mwazva here ana mai Wiribheti namai Giribheti. Kuti muri kuda kumbondizwawo munoreketa zvakanaka, zviro ngezvekuwirirana nekureketerana mwazva here?*' I had blurted out.

Amainini Rusiya chose to be diplomatic when she confronted me with the rumour that had swept across the sprawling suburb. Our affair was no longer a secret, but a public secret that had sailed into the public domain.

A number of my friends were beginning to glorify me and showing signs of joining the bandwagon. In a desperate bid to stem the tide of a morale decadency, their parents forbade them from associating with me, threatening them with banishment to their tribal trust lands.

But teenagers full of adventures to explore into unknown territories, would always find a way to skirt around those threats. Some would shower me with some gifts expressing their allegiance and loyalty. Suddenly, I had become a cult hero.

For those who kept pestering me about their intention to engage in sexual activities with older women and older girls, I would pimp them to those willing to service them, of course for a fee.

That was how I became a pimp. I would arrange venues for the boys and their catches. Before long a number of bigger boys who attended local secondary schools and young men who were working for various companies in the Eastern border city, would come knocking at my door for my pimping services.

To silence Amainini Rusiya, I would arrange some quickies for her during her live-in boyfriend's absence.

Her business roared to prowling levels, so did mine. I also enlisted the services of some *sangomas* who earned their keeps through hawking traditional herbs like aphrodisiacs and those that cured various sexual transmitted diseases known then as *siki* or *njovhera*.

CHAPTER 46

DARLING OF THE HOOD

I had turned into a darling of the hood overnight. I would bed some young and vivacious single mothers and older girls from the hood in return for my pimping services. Those ones offered better services than Amai Charisi who was sauntering on the verge of becoming a sunset.

Age, poverty, sexual escapades and children that she had ushered into this world by the gross, were beginning to take their toll on her. I was beginning to detest the smell of her children's urine and milk since she was lactating.

I just could not stand the site of the two. Due to grinding poverty, she would sometimes bath without a cake of soap. Instead, she would resort to using the traditional soap, which she would have imported from her tribal trust land.

As if that was not enough, she could not afford to apply some lightening creams like Ambi and Ponds. Her wardrobe left a lot to be desired. She acquired most of her clothes from a crude tailor who operated from Murapa Tavern. As had become her modus operandi, the lethargic and out of sorts tailor was added to her dwindling list of boyfriends. I would hang around at entrances of Murapa Tavern, Mushando Bar, Maonde Bar as well as Nyausunzi Bar in the company of some smartly dressed young women, gyrating to some music blaring from some Jukeboxes.

We would jive, engage in chips and twist types of dances that involved the seductive twisting and turning of the waist. The ladies would be clad in latest fashion trends then. All of the girls who would go to great lengths just to appear like *vana misis* or *madhamu*, white belles, would be wafting with some expensive colognes.

The ladies sophisticated as they appeared to be, would imbibe in *masese* from *mugojo*. There they would drown their sorrows taking sips and swigs from some white mugs.

They would wipe their mouths off *masese* with the back of their hands. The fortunate ones would wipe their mouths and blow their noses with handkerchiefs.

Those who were obsessed with modernity would puff away cigarette smoke into the atmosphere through artificial gaps between their teeth.

They would dangle some big earrings known as *madhikausi*. I got to hear the swishing sounds of beads which adorn waists of most women worth their salts. The young women would compete with each other to spoil me with soft drinks, *zviponda moyo* and *makendikeke*. After all, I held the keys to their survival. I was living large for my age. I wielded a lot of power and influence for my age. Power is sweet and absolute power corrupts the mind.

I would move around with two henchmen for my protection. With my stocks soaring, with each flirting day, I began to date Amai Giribheti and Amai Wiribheti.

I would visit the two in the company of my armour bearers who would keep guard during my amorous acts. With the passage of time, my relationships with the two ladies became the talk of the hood.

CHAPTER 47

ARMOUR BEARERS

The two women's husbands sought to beat me up, but they could not as my armour bearers kept me under guard. By then, I had moved to Muchena where I shared a room with my armour bearers. I had ceased hanging around with my age-mates.

I no longer frequented the John Fisher Dam, an abandoned quarry behind Mwamuka Shopping Complex. When days were dark, I used to jostle with other boys from the hood fishing for the pot.

I no longer spent my weekends playing hide and seek near Hilltop Mountain. I no longer passed my time watching some unsuspecting couples engaging in sexual acts in the bush mountain behind Hilltop church. I no longer partook in *mutserendende, mudzuwerere,* swings or the sprinkling of *uriri* in some small dams where we used to swim. I had since stopped backstroking and butterflying in the affluent Sakubva River where industrial wastes were discharged in abundance. I no longer ate sadza with *Konorosi*, a type of relish that grew on the riverbanks of Sakubva River. I no longer engaged in the obscene graffiti writing of public lavatories using our own excreta. Then toilet paper was expensive and a preserve for whites.

The majority of blacks in the townships would resort to using old newspapers, maize cobs or worse still the naughty ones would use their bare hands to wipe clean their behinds.

Some traces of the human excreta known in Korekore as *chitsvodzo* would be left stuck and dry on our shorts, which would be badly patched, or worse still would show our backsides through some gaping holes.

We would wear our shirts or *sikipas* until our bodies could be seen through. Ironically, those were the days of see-through women outfits that needed to be complemented with some nylon or *kirimbirini* colourful petticoats or the heavy brands known as *mubvara dhongi.*

We would visit lavatories and communal bathrooms bare footed. We would take showers whilst chewing at cakes of soaps for they were a *delicacy* and scarce. *Pata patas* were a luxury then. The fortunate ones would sport some homemade sandals known as *hwasho* or *tsapata*.

Trapping birds with *urimbo* or worse still shooting them down ferociously with catapults crafted from black power was no longer part of my lifestyle. We used to symbolize the shooting down of birds with catapults to the downing of the Rhodesian Airforce's bombers by freedom fighters. That really inspired us a lot. Then we would engage in shooting exercises like the ones soldiers hold at Gimboki Shooting Range near Dangamvura.

I no longer took part in *sarura wako, dhere, laka laka, chuti, tsoro yemakomba, draft, tsetsetse, pada, dunhu, njuga, makasi, scotch, fongo, smart bhabhi, chisveru, dzvambu* and *chabuta.* I no longer passed my time helping ice-cream vendors in wheeling and pushing their tri-cycles for a few pats on the back.

I no longer dangled for free rides on the carriers of buses that plied the hood's routes. I no longer used to dice for free rides at the back of Council tippers that would bring some gravel for road construction.

I no longer teamed up with some boys from the hood in the stealing of some green mangoes and peaches from the hood. The green *mabhuru* mangoes, which we would munch at hungrily, went down well with course salt, which was cheaper and believed to be saltier by blackest township dwellers.

Apart from being cheaper, course salt was also used as *chifumuro* that is it was used to neutralize traditional charms.

I had since stopped playing *gweshe,* I no longer poked fun at refuse collectors, public toilet cleaners or engaged in public spats with some deranged men and women from the hood.

I had since stopped in partaking in money games at Murapa Tavern where I had become the toast of the venue. Instead, I would take to the plunges at Sakubva Swimming Pool, engage in slug encounters, flipper as well as frequenting Sakubva Beit Hall for cinemas or bioscope.

I would also pay for my entrance and that of my armour bearers into Sakubva Stadium then an impregnable fortress of the now defunct Umtali United whose goals were kept by Proud *Kilimanjalo* Chinembiri who never conceded a single goal in the goal behind Munowenyu Shopping Complex. Chinembiri went on to become Africa's heavyweight pugilist champion.

CHAPTER 48

JOY SEEKERS

I would literally run shows at jukeboxes where I would not allow any reveller or night crawler to crawl rhythmically to my choice of music.

Then I had fallen in love with rhumba from the then Zaire, kanindo, and sungura from East African countries like Kenya and Tanzania.

Bioscope then was something else. We could detect the scent of gunpowder off the big screen. We would root for the likes of Bruce Lee, Anna Mao, Jimmy Kelly, Chuck Norris and Mas Villa with all our might. We would shout *Iwe, Iwe* whenever our heroes landed punches or kicks on their opponents.

Then *maguruvhas* or *zhoris* would always be the fall guys. They would always be pummelled into submission. We would also watch some cartoons or the likes of Charlie Chaplin.

Those who could not afford to pay for their entries into Sakubva Beit Hall would assist the cinema guys with some manual jobs. Some boys would sell of some bones to bone collectors.

Then we blindly believed that those bones were ground into powder to make some porcelain cups and saucers *cup nendiro dzevhu* or *dongo* or *dhaga*. A vehicle from Van de Burgh would move around collecting bones.

Then I dreamt of mixing and mingling with whites at Umtali's Drive Inn where motorists used to watch movies in the comfort of their vehicles.

That Drive Inn was situated at an area that was adjacent to Bernwin and Brian James' farm *kwaBhuru* along Magamba Drive that linked Hobhouse and Fairbridge Park.

To diversify my business, I would supply vendors who thronged schools in the hood with food and sweets. These would sell for a commission.

I also became a shebeen king and a money launderer using my

armour bearers as debt collectors. I would throw some Society Parties and things would be sold at inflated prices.

Music would only be played upon special request. Those gifted with sublime dancing skills would retire home with bulging pockets as revellers would place bets on them so as to spur them to out dance each other.

Using the power vested in me by my armour bearers, I would force patrons who frequented Sakubva's watering holes to pay protection fees if they wanted to enjoy their peace. I had mutated into a self-proclaimed master of some sort. I had the freedom to move around harassing patrons who would not have complied, taking away meat, which they would have been roasting at braai stands.

I would provoke and pick a fight with any man who would be in the company of a beautiful lady. I would prey on any beautiful lady in the hood.

No woman would turn down my advances since turning down my proposal would result in that woman's husband being beaten into a bloody pulp.

Fearing for their safety and that of their wives and children, a number of men sent their families back to their kraals where some kraal heads would have field days ploughing into them with their ploughshares.

I also had the power to declare anybody who would have crossed my path, a Prohibited Immigrant.

With the money I was making, I could afford to send my siblings to school as well as fend for our mother who had landed a job at Bhuru's Farm near Drive Inn.

As time flirted by, my affection for Amai Charisi died a natural death. But the aging married woman would not have any of that and sought to fix me.

At first, she volunteered information to Baba Giribheti and Baba Wiribheti to the effect that I had become an item with their wives.

Upon realizing that the duo could not get to confront me since I had become a law unto myself, she tipped the Sakubva Rural Police Station on the type of business I was running in Maonde.

By then I had diversified into selling some drugs like *mbanje* and *ganja* cakes. Fortunately, a police officer who received the tip-off was one of those who lived off my sweat. I quickly moved my contraband to a safe haven, a cave in a mountain near Devonshire. I vowed to hit back at Amai Charisi with the vengeance of a black mamba.

Six months later, I took Charisi and Joromiya to that bush of *madhorosiya* behind the United Methodist Hilltop Assembly, which Amai Charisi and Baba Joromiya had converted into their permanent love nest. I had lied to Charisi and Joromiya that I wanted to take them to an area where they could trap some guinea fowls.

When we arrived at the so-called guinea fowl playing ground, Baba Joromiya aka Amukaka and Amai Charisi's love nest and rendezvous, we hid behind some shrubs.

CHAPTER 49

TAKING TO FLIGHT

In no time, Amai Charisi and Baba Joromiya arrived for another series of steamy sessions. They made love to a point where both Joromiya and Charisi could not withstand the sight of their amorous parents.

The pair who were armed with catapults and knobkerries, challenged their parents before pelting them with pebbles as I watched gaily from a distance. The adulterous pair who were in Adamaic and Eveic suits, took to flight with Joromiya and Charisi hot in pursuit.

In no time, the entire neighbourhood was ears agog and awash with news of an adulterous duo that had been caught in the act. A mob that had converged and swelled with the passage of time, resolved to mete out an instant mob justice. The mob that had been angered with the pair's monkeyshines, started to hurl some stones at the naked pair.

The crowd that was pelting the duo with stones whilst continuously baying for their blood, continued to swell into a massive throng. Among those who were attracted by the throng was Amai Joromiya and Baba Charisi. In no time, all hell had broken loose. Amai Joromiya furiously descended on Amai Charisi whilst at the same time an enraged Baba Charisi pummelled a bemused Baba Joromiya into a bloody pulp. Amai Charisi who had been given a thumping of her life, owned up to the true paternity of her children.

She made a confession to the effect that none of her children were sired by Baba Charisi. The crowd cried for the blood of the butcher boy, the grinder, Amukaka the milkman and Madzibaba Crynage the prophet.

The milkman, butcher boy and the grinder were given a hiding of a lifetime. Angry as the crowd appeared to be, it exercised restraint towards Madzibaba Crynage. Nobody could lift a finger against the self-proclaimed prophet. Those in attendance feared his supernatural powers.

The commotion attracted the police who came and bundled the quartet into their marked Land Rover before wheeling them to Umtali Rural Police Station.

At the station, four dockets were opened, two for indecent exposure against Baba Joromiya and Amai Charisi and the other two for serious bodily harm.

Charges of grievously bodily harm were levelled against Baba Charisi and Amai Joromiya. Following that hullabaloo, the police launched a massive crackdown against women who were illegally staying in Sakubva.

A lot of women and children were swooped in the net that had been cast far and wide by the Smith establishment. Those who were arrested were released after paying admission of guilty fines.

Those who could not raise the gazetted or rather stipulated fines were arraigned before the courts to answer charges of staying in the hood illegally. Some were branded Prohibited Immigrants.

Amainini Rusiya moved base to McGreggors. Amai Charisi, Amai Joromiya and a plethora of other women were some of those caught in the web. Amai Charisi's marriage crumpled whilst Amai Joromiya retraced her footsteps to Baba Joromiya's rural home of Bocha.

The country had not yet attained independence. Only women who were employed at Sunlow had the right to be in Sakubva in which the majority of houses were intended for black men. The system then did not allow black men to stay in cities and towns with their wives and children. African women were then confined to the rural areas. African men then would only visit their spouses once a year at Christmas holidays.

CHAPTER 50

THE LITMUS TEST

Legend has it that then, African women were not allowed to wash their privates during their husbands' absence. The husbands would want to stick it out in the sticky honey pot when they reported home for their annual conjugal rights.

That stickiness was a sure sign of faithfulness. That stickiness could be equated to the chastity lock that was used by sailors who always kept their spouses under lock and key whenever they set sail across vast acres of waters in voyages.

It was taboo for African women to shave off their privates without their husbands' consent and knowledge. That shave done behind their husbands' back resulted in divorces.

That shave which women of today full of their airs and big words, might view as misdemeanours and a routine health makeover, resulted in kangaroo courts that involved aunts being hastily convened.

Teenage girls were expected to go through the bedroom mill, where they were initiated into womanhood. During those initiation ceremonies, the girls would be required to go through virginity testing that involved water or egg testing. An egg would be pushed into their privates through their thighs as they would be lying facing the sky with legs astride.

This is the reason why some churches still use the egg to test for virginity on the very day those about to wed are to be led down the aisle. That fragile egg could be a source of protein, joy, triumphant and embarrassment. Virginity that could have been lost within some seconds and behind closed doors or in the bush, could turn out to be public talk as well as haunting the victim for life.

Any woman worth her salt would have taken pride in the elongation of their labia. Some went to the extent of using snuff like *bute* or *mudhombo*. Legend has it that when the woman sneezed, the labia would also increase in length and size. And legend had it then that the thickness of a woman's lips determined the thickness of her labia. Women were expected to adorn their waists with different shades of beads. *Usanga* and labia were regarded as men's toys during foreplay.

Some women would go to great lengths to please their men by having *nyora* on their thighs or the area that lead to the oasis of joy. The incisions, which would be rubbed with some herbs that had the arousal effect on men, was known as *starters*.

Whilst women could lie fallow waiting to be ploughed during the rainy season, bulls had the freedom to stray out of their kraals in search of single women. These were deliberately employed so that they could keep men entertained as they drowned their sorrows in Council beer gardens dotted across neighbourhoods.

These sharpened the ploughshares in readiness for the rainy season, in readiness for those fields that would have laid fallow in anticipation of uncontaminated and heavy rains.

Family planning methods then were a preserve of the white minority who wanted to keep their families within their means whilst indirectly encouraging blacks to increase their labour force.

African women would rely on natural ways of family planning like breast-feeding which wasn't effective hence a lot of infants succumbed to diseases that came with being breastfed with contaminated milk.

Some African women would tie some strings around their waists that would have been yarned or coiled from some traditional herbs. Legend has it that women who used that method would only fall pregnant, once that string got yanked resulting in snapping.

Condoms, known as Durex, were the new man in town, were a preserve for whites. Condoms were associated with loose characters as Paul Matavire would call them, '*Zviro zviya zvandakapihwa nema nurse ndakarasa, mbuya we ndakuvara, mbuya we ndakuvara.*' Condoms were alien and unheard off.

CHAPTER 51

UP IN SMOKE

I woke up with a start, the same start that you would have if you were to wake up under siege from some blood sucking and serrated blood dripping vampires. I could hear some heavy footsteps and the cocking of automatic rifles. When I heard those sounds, I knew my world had crumbled around me. My game was up in smoke. The empire that I had laboured to establish was in danger of collapsing.

My reign in the hood was surely coming to an abrupt end, a reign that I was still enjoying. I also heard the sounds of some sniffing dogs, dogs that had been trained in drug sniffing. Beads of sweat swiftly formed on my forehead.

A deluge of sweat started to cascade down my body in rivulets that had been triggered with fear and terror. I was petrified to the core of the bone marrow. As I was still engaged in a wrestling contest with my racing thoughts, a tear-smoke canister was hurled through a broken windowpane chocking us in the process. I could see my armour bearers reeling and writhing in agony. Tears trickled down their faces like torrential floods. The tear-smoke was slowly taking its effect. Before long, we all appeared marooned by its effects.

A white police officer, *mujoni,* who was in charge of the operation, *Operation Restoration,* lunged at the door with all the force he could muster, ripping it off its hinges. The imposing *mujoni* stood at the doorway with arms akimbo.

His towering figure appeared ominous and snarling. A service pistol that dangled from its upholstery sent our hearts leaping into our mouths. My most efficient and ruthless armour bearer Sauro was sent reeling against the wall by the *mujoni.*

Before he could crash land with a thud, he was caught on the hip with a ferocious kick that could have seen Jean Claude turning green with envy. By the time he crash-landed on the floor, he had already spoiled his pants with excreta. Urine cascaded down his trousers. My armour bearers and I were bundled into a police Jeep. The house, which we had turned into a haven of various contrabands of narcotics and illicit brews, was turned inside-out by the police.

They had brought in a pack of vicious dogs trained in narcotics sniffing. They ransacked my lodgings leaving it in a mess of strews. A myriad of clothes was left strewn all over the room that we had tried to keep as tidy as possible.

Satisfied by their catch as well as the evidence that they had gathered, they jeeped us to Sakubva Police Station. There, plethoras of charges were levelled against us. The gravity of the charges that were preferred against us began to sink in. We dismally and technically failed to build alibis. A myriad of defences that we would have laboured to build came crushing against us.

I was sentenced to ten strokes, which were to be administered on me by a Probation Officer at Umtali's Probation Centre near Umtali Teachers College whilst my armour bearers were each slapped with an effective six months' custodial sentence.

At Umtali Prison Farm, *Panguruve*, they served their time. I was saved from being slapped with a custodial sentence due to my age. Upon the completion of my sentence, I was released into the care of Amainini Rusiya.

I had lost quite a fortune during the raid. Some unscrupulous police officers who had stumbled upon a cache of the Rhodesian currency that I had stashed away in a mattress, had helped themselves to the loot.

That impacted negatively on my status which had evolved over a very short period of time. I had curved a niche for myself in the underworld business. I had dreamed of having contacts from the Middle East and Colombia where I intended to transact with Pablo Escobar's gang. I had also dreamed of keeping in constant touch with Italy's Mafia. I woke up from that big deep slumber of a nightmare drenched to the bone under a deluge of sweat. The nightmare served one purpose. It galvanized me into activating my security details. No matter how hard I tried to avert the passing of that nightmare, it finally came to pass.

CHAPTER 52

SUN SET

I had a premonition that something sinister was lurking in my way. The nightmare pointed to Amai Charisi who was out to even scores with me. I had played a fast one on her. She had been thrown out of her matrimonial house on to the streets.

Prostitution was no longer lucrative to her. Age had finally caught up with her. Her multiple clients who used to queue at her doorstep for their feel and fill, were dwindling down. Even Amukaka the milkman, the butcher boy, the grinder, Madzibaba Crynage and Mufundisi were no longer attracted to her.

She had over the years lost her charm. Besides, none of the men was prepared to commit themselves to a woman of such loose morals, a harlot. None of those men was prepared even to co-habit with Amai Charisi.

None of those men was prepared to fend for a woman who had made bad news in the community, not once, not twice, not thrice, but on a number of times the community had lost count of. Hanging around with the aging porn star attracted a raucous of laughter, a round of sneers and a barrage of jeers. She had become a laughing stock in Sakubva. No man worth his salt would dare to flirt around with her for he too risked becoming a joint laughing stock.

Two days later, Amai Charisi darkened my residence where she created a scene. She vowed never to leave my lodgings for she claimed that she was my official wife. She told those within earshot that she had sacrificed her marriage in a bid to placate and satiate my sexual libido.

As if that was not enough, she claimed I had masterminded the breakup of her marriage to Baba Charisi by blowing her cover.

When I tried to dispute the fact that I had slept with her, she pulled up her skirt, exposed her backside and some shiny beads, which she claimed, always kept me engrossed in the subsistence of our affair.

To add credence to her claims, she took off her pair of tattered and torn under garment, which she used to strike me on the face with.

'Bhurugwa iri haurizive here? Hauziriwe wakandibvarurira ndichiramba kurara newe here uchiti waizonditengera?'

That was the last thing I wanted to hear. I turned around, looked on the ground before covering my face with my hands. That accusation was sweet music to the ears of my neighbours and those who had gathered to witness a free live drama. Muffled giggles, sneers and jeers filled the atmosphere.

For a moment, nobody from the throng could recall that I was one of the ghetto's most feared thug who moved around with armour bearers flaunting and flexing their muscles.

I had been reduced to a mere teenager. I was no longer the teenager who used to wield so much influence in the sprawling suburb. I was no longer the teenager who used to instil fear into residents from our community.

I had been reduced to size by an aging hooker, a shameless harlot who was out to settle scores with me.

I had been taken by surprise by Amai Charisi's actions. They the armour bearers had also been astounded by Amai Chari's actions, actions that had left the hood in both shock and awe.

Prior to Amai Charisi's indecent exposure that exposed our shenanigans, nobody from the hood could dare to accuse me of dating Amai Charisi or any other married woman.

The leveling of such accusations against the ghetto's cult hero could lead to banishment from the hood or worse still Umtali, the city.

CHAPTER 53

STAGE MANAGING MIRACLES

There was a time when I could force an entire section to attend a church service at a church whose pastor or founder could have paid me to coerce members from the community to attend their services. I also used to be paid to stage manage some healing miracles.

I can vividly recall this other Super Sunday when I was hired by Super Highway Pentecostal Church to ape a lunatic. I acted like a deranged man for a week. During that week, I feasted on food that would have been strategically dumped in refuse bins.

I smeared myself with some charcoal and ashes. I would mumble and hurl some obscenities at passers-by who would stop from time to time just to get a glimpse of me. Nobody really sympathize with me for I was a menace who had hounded them into their shells.

Most members of the community whom I had dealt with ruthlessly in the past all believed that my sins had caught up with me.

Some aggrieved husbands whose wives he snared bewitched him. He is also paying the price for devilish deeds. We knew all along that one day he would meet his match. There was a time when some church leaders would hire me to cause chaos to their rivals. I would unleash my armour bearers on pastors just to scatter the sheep. I would threaten to return the following Sunday during service to deal ruthlessly with any dissenting voices.

That way, a number of promising churches closed shop fearing for the worst. Only churches of founders who would have greased my palms with some dirty money would be allowed to operate. I was a law unto myself. I was a Saul reincarnate.

I would unleash violence against Christians all at the instigation of anti-Christ. I was a merchant of the devil or worse still, a devil incarnate. Fetish priests feared me, *sangomas* feared me, witches and wizards feared me also.

The devil also feared me for my devilish acts had defied satanic acts. Satanists or those who dabbled in the Illuminati world also feared me. I was as fearless as a Queen of the Waters from the marine underworld.

The words fear and fearless feared me for I had times without number badgered them into compliance. Such was my diabolic influence. I remember one gloomy day when I forced a prominent prophet to eat his excreta in full glare of his congregants, having strong-armed him with the aid of my armour bearers.

Upon my release from the reformatory institution, I had no means of survival. I turned to crime and formed a gang that terrorised the Sakubva community. The reign of terror that I had unleashed into the hood, continued unabated into independence. At independence, I joined the then newly established Youth Brigade.

I swiftly rose through the ranks to become youth chairman which incorporated all the community's wards. I would unleash some members of the youth's brigade, most of who had criminal traits, on my perceived enemies. I became a law unto myself.

Education was made free by the new government, which was premiered by Cde Robert Mugabe. I could not take advantage of the generous system that intended to empower blacks academically.

Several youths who had dropped out of school due to a myriad of challenges joined the swelling bandwagon of those who had taken advantage of the government's initiative.

Those who had sought refuge in neighbouring countries and ex-combatants who had been demobilised from the force as well as those who had been enlisted into the Zimbabwe National Army, enrolled with a plethora of educational institutions that catered for adult education.

Several study groups and night schools were established by the new regime to advance the education cause under Minister Dzingai Mutumbuka. I had enrolled at Alpha Study Group, which operated in Sakubva.

I found the going tough and soon fell by the wayside, as I could not grasp most of the concepts. I became a laughing stock. That saw me clashing with several of my classmates. To save face, I withdrew from the study group to concentrate on party business. I went through the rigorous training at Nyanga's Battalion Battle School in which we were taught martial arts tactics that strengthened our self-defence mechanisms. That training suited my pugnaciousness character.

It awakened the bellicosity demon that lay in me. I was later integrated into Masvingo's Fourth Brigade. I saw action along Zimbabwe's border with Mozambique where our brigade kept the rogue Renamo bandits at bay.

I was also involved in battles against Renamo at Gorongoza and Cassa Banana in Mozambique, went for peacekeeping duties in Somalia and Angola before being deployed into the jungles of the Democratic Republic of Congo where President Laurent Desiree Kabila was under siege from some marauding rebels.

I proved my mettle in the equatorial rain forests of Goma, Bujumayi and in areas just outside Kinshasa. I gallantly fought in defence of our country's all weather friend.

I rose through the rank of a Lieutenant Colonel. The rank was conferred to me following a series of victories over the rebels that were being allegedly propped by some Western countries.

CHAPTER 54

THE RAID

Heavy rattling sounds of gunfire thundered on the dilapidated building of our ramshackle makeshift camp that was under rebel siege. When the second knocking rattled against the building threatening to rip it from her foundation, I wormed out of my warm sleeping bag that had gone off colour, as if from an automatic assault rifle.

Beads of sweat that had formed on my forehead trickled down my swarthy body in rivulets that culminated into a deluge that soaked me to the bone. I had just not emerged from a nightmare. This was real.

Rebels who were determined to overrun our camp in Goma had delivered the spitting sounds of guns that had jerked me into life. Before launching the attack, the rebels had sabotaged power lines that supplied electricity to the camp, plunging it into an abyss of darkness.

So gloomy was the night that even phantoms would fear to ghost about in their phantom business.

The previous raid effected at the crack of dawn on the same camp two months back, had seen quite a number of casualties in the Congolese Army which was caught unawares. The rebels had almost successfully overran that camp until my platoon was called in to reinforce the Congolese Army whose pockets of resistance were almost broken. We called in our Airforce, which responded swiftly at the crack of dawn.

In a flash, the friendly forces had turned the tables against the rebels who were retreating towards a mighty river that was gurgling and frothing with foaming water. Under siege from the friendly forces who had encircled them and pressing them against the river, they had no choice, but to seek refugee into the cold and dark waters of the river.

Most of the rebels drowned in the river in which hippos and crocodiles lurked. In no time, the belly of the river that appeared to possess a colossal appetite swallowed most of the rebels.

Another large number of the rebels were killed as we gallantly repelled their attack at the camp. Only a handful of our forces were killed in defence of our camp. They had gallantly died in action. We had taken a few prisoners of war whom we kept hostages at our camp.

A good number of rebels' bodies floated in the river. These were rebels who had not seen the wisdom of giving in to the mighty friendly forces who were cool, calm and calculated in the execution of the war. The rebels had asked for a war and we were simply taking the war to them.

This was a war and a war is no child's play. In any war, blood is bound to be shed, flow in abundance and lives are bound to be lost. Casualties are bound to be lost. Those who find themselves on the receiving end of any war are bound to be economic with the truth with regards to the actual number of casualties. Morale is bound to sink to an all-time low or soar to its highest ebb.

Friends and foes are lost, survive and spared. Tears of joy and anguish are shed. The sign of victory as well as the sign of villain would be shown and raised.

CHAPTER 55

THE RIVER BETWEEN

As we lay crammed in the cell of Mutare Remand Prison that had been plunged into an abyss of darkness, a dungeon of despair, memories of how my friend Dhakota's wife was gang raped by a marauding and rogue gang of *gombiros* came flooding my mind.

Gombiros were gem robbers, those who used their muscles to instil fear into industrious *gwejas*. They were an equivalence of rank Marshalls and pirates or buccaneers, sea robbers.

They are the law, they make laws, they break laws and they float above the law. Some of these *gombiros* instil laws onto law enforcement agents and lawyers.

Dorica had been hired to cook for a gang of *gwejas* from Shurugwi who had set up their base at Zengeni in Bocha. She had carried out the job perfectly well. Things came to a point when Dorica demanded payment for the services she had rendered.

The notorious gang that was under the leadership of the brawny Ten Boy, sent her from pillar to post with innumerable promises that were never fulfilled. Drugged and tired of the *gwejas's* promises and lies, Dorica whose husband had been absorbed into the *Gunners* Syndicate that prowled Mutaka *waMai Yafa Mari*, resolved to stay put at the gang's makeshift camp until her debt was serviced in full.

She stayed put up to around 10 pm. Unknowingly, she was playing into the hands of the diabolic *gwejas* who had been sexually starved for weeks on end.

She vowed to put up for the night at the *gwejas'* camp, but was told in no certain terms to leave or be sexually abused. With a heavy heart, Dorica stormed out into the night that cast tongues of some grotesque silhouettes.

She had an intuition that something bad was going to befall her as she trudged back to Mufakose where her husband's gang was camped having moved from an area known to *gwejas* and *gwejelines* as on the TV.

The volume of *gwejas* who were going into the diamond fields had thickened. Most *gwejas* and *gwejelines* preferred to plunge into tunnels where they would slug it out with some *migwaras* in the *gwejas* parlance.

Only a few *gwejas* who were under the influence of dagga or *dzemabhinya dzakafudhubhaiwa* would scale the razor wire in broad daylight to mine in what was known as *Live Show yaMacheso*.

As she approached a huge baobob tree near *Mufombi*, which had become a haven for *magombiros*, her heart skipped when six silhouetted figures strategically surrounded her.

A voice that Dorica suspected to be that of Ten Boy bombarded her with questions. Two members of the gang demanded sex from her. She pleaded with the duo not to abuse her sexually as she was a married woman. Her pleas drew a raucous laughter from the pair who tore her clothes to shreds leaving her in the nude.

Her distress calls were muffled with a gag that was tied to her mouth. The two took turns to rape her, inserting their menhoods in almost every orifice. The other four joined in the savage sexual attack that left her bleeding profusely. They only left her when she passed out.

Raped without protection, Dorica was later picked up by another group of *gwejas* who were coming from the fields with sackfuls of *mutaka* or samples. A report was filed with the police.

However, no docket was opened as some buyers of the gems swiftly moved in to protect Ten Boy and his gang, which always supplied them with good quality gems known as *maclear, magirazi* or *ngwetungwetu isina chipomerwa*.

None of the gang members were arraigned before the courts even after Dorica had positively identified three of them. The police insisted it was a case of mistaken identity. When Dhakota returned from the fields, he desperately tried to have the perpetrators brought to book, but his efforts came crushing against a brick wall, so did the case that he laboured to build. The police were determined to sweep the case under the carpet as well as perpetuating the alleged rapists' freedom.

The couple was left to rue the day they thought of venturing into Chiadzwa diamond fields where Dorica had made a killing by hawking food.

Tears of frustration trickled down my cheeks threatening to erode my dimples. Floodgates of sweat meandered down my body from every pore, leaving me soaked to the marrow.

I was shaking with anger whilst at the same time wincing in excruciating pain. A fresh wound inflicted by a razor sharp teeth of a police dog Bruno that had lacerated through my calf leaving a deep cut, pierced through my heart.

I had escaped from a barrage of *mosibhegi*, *chifefe* from some trigger-happy police officers on horsebacks. This was a combined operation that involved the police's *Gondo Harishayi* and the Army who were being backed by the Airforce.

Mosibhegi was a type of weapon used by the police's reaction team to scare away *gwejas* from diamond fields in Chiadzwa. The weapon was not lethal, but was capable of discharging some minute shrapnels that were painful and effective in reducing the mobility of *gwejas*.

The operation that was carried out in 2008 was code named *Gweja Dzoka Kumba*. Those who were nabbed were ordered by the police to sing *Gweja dzoka kumba mai vako vari kudana, Gweja dzoka kumba.*

The officers who we had previously referred to as *vana vehanzvadzi dzedu* had departed from leading those they would have arrested into singing *Jehova ndibatsireiwo pandimire pakaoma baba, Jehova ndibatsireiwo baba pandimire pakaoma...*

Previously, we had urged police officers to continue firing salvos of bullets into the sky as the sounds of gunfire sounded melodiously. *Muzaya ramba uchiridza pfuti nditambe.*

The dog that had been unleashed upon me, only got to loosen his grip on my calf after I had struck him with a metal bar known in the *makorokozas'* phraseology as *mugwara.*

He had whimpered away to his handler. I had sprinted towards Odzi River where some crocodiles lurked in wait for us *gwejas*. Suddenly, I was under attack from a crocodile. It serrated through into the same calf that had been mauled by Bruno earlier on. I had to sink the metal rod into its mouth.

The lethal reptile had tasted blood and was determined to fight hard for its supper. We had been ordered by a team of *gombiros* under *The*

Terminator to form a human barrier against both crocodiles and the frothing Odzi River.

We were made to hold our hands together as we wadded, wriggled, wiggled into the gurgling and frothing Odzi River, the river between Odzi and Chiadzwa.

The human barrier was broken when I came under siege from the crocodile attack, which I tenaciously and viciously fought with the aplomb of a once marooned commando in the Democratic Republic of Congo.

That crocodile siege claimed one victim, a certain Hezero from Masvingo's Chesvingo suburb. A single mother of a two-year-old Kupakwashe who was comfortably tucked away at the back of *The Terminator*, Hezero had lost her footing after I came under attack from the crocodile.

She had desperately tried to clutch on to some straws, but the frothing and gurgling river had gurgled her away into her belly where she became supper for crocodiles. After I had recovered from the shock of my encounter with the reptile and having wadded myself to safety, I was told of the washing away of Hezero.

I wept uncontrollably for Hezero. I blamed myself for her painful death. I could not imagine her banging her beautiful face and intelligent head against some rugged and jagged boulders that awaited to embrace her into the gloomy belly of the river.

I could not imagine the beautifully shaped Hezero, an embodiment of beauty, a paragon of etiquette, an oasis of resilience and hope, being swallowed by the belly of the river.

I could not imagine the former Masvingo City belle being ravaged, rummaged and devoured by the serrated blood suckling reptiles that prowled the river keeping gwejas under check and siege.

I just could not fathom to imagine Hezero the smiley one, smiling her way into the belly of the insatiable, cruel and callous river with a roaring gargantuan appetite. I just could not imagine myself losing a community belle who was beginning to warm up to my advances. I could still feel the warmth and smoothness of her palms.

I could still feel the softness of her cherubic baby face. Her skin was as smooth as a parrot's breast to the touch, radiant, blinding and dazzling to the eye. That was Hezero, my newly found love, lover and loveliest. By the banks of the river between, I shed tears in memory of Hezero.

I swiftly fished out one of my best shirts that I had bought from Chipindirwi's makeshift shops, tore it to smithereens and used it to tie my calf as I battled to stop blood from oozing out.

I was then beginning to feel the effects of the wound. I had lost quite a lot of blood and that influenced my progress.

That impact cascaded into the entire team that had to slow down to match mine. Then I was hobbling with a limp like the much-feared Long John Silver of the famed *Treasure Island*.

I had to walk with the aid of a rugged walking stick that appeared to be in agreement with the jagged terrain. I continued to shed tears of migration whilst at the same time nursing a wound I had picked during *Operation Gweja Dzoka Kumba*. As we camped to allow for my recuperation, I just could not imagine darkness enveloping the atmosphere without Hezero. I found solace in her daughter Kupakwashe who was being cuddled away by Hezero's friend Yivhoni.

Shattered, I drifted into dreamland. I could faintly hear the gurgling and frothing sound of the river between, a constant reminder of how the devilish river had nibbled and masticated away my Hezero. Little did we know that a few yards behind us lay the lifeless body of Hezero who had been thrown up by the gurgling, swirling and frothing river.

I guessed Hezero wanted to keep watch over Kupakwashe, her daughter. Her eyes, which yearned for true love and true happiness, shone with contagious love, love of the common people. They beamed with optimism and pliability. Even in her death, she could not stop smiling. Even in the face of death, death from an unlikely source, the river between, she still could afford a contagious smile.

Even when staring death in the face and without her two most prized assets, her daughter Kupakwashe and I, she surprisingly glared and gleaned at the cruel world, a world that had deliberately and callously weaned her from the real world.

Her clothes were tattered and torn, shredded and shrivelled. I wailed for the lifeless body of Hezero. All she could do was to smile at me, a contagious smile.

Although she could no longer talk, she remained defiant and committed to her daughter and me. She remained mum like a mummified figure. After mourning myself beyond gutted levels, I slumped into another bout of slumber, a big deep sleep of my creator, my maker. I was awakened by some moans and groans consistent with those attached to love making. I later realized that it was *The Terminator* and his two accomplices who had forced themselves on three defenceless and hapless women in our group.

One of them called Ndiringe sickly made attempts at Yivhoni who was protecting Kupakwashe. Yivhoni tried to use Kupakwashe to block Ndiringe's advances, but he would have none of that.

Angered by Yivhoni's tricks of using Kupakwashe as a shield to scuttle his efforts to force himself on her, Ndiringe wrestled the luckless Kupakwashe from Yivhoni's vice like grip and threw her into the river.

Her wails were drowned by the frothing river as she was made to join her departed mother. Shocked by the cruelty displayed by Ndiringe, Yivhoni let out a piercing scream that sliced through the forest disturbing the serenity and tranquillity that had been reigning supreme.

We all rushed to Yivhoni's aid only to be stopped dead in our tracks by Ndiringe who had drawn a razor sharp machete that shone under the moonlight.

We all backtracked as Ndiringe threatened to knife anyone who dared to challenge him. He was really spoiling for a real and bloody fight. His two accomplices, who had been raping other women, sprang to his aid.

They too were armed to the teeth with some machetes and okapi knives. Fear gripped us. We were shepherded into a thicket, far from where the petrified trio of women they had singled out were huddled half-naked.

The sixteen of us were ransacked, pockets were turned inside out. We were later ordered to say out our last prayers. Instead of saying out our last prayers piously, we all begged the trio to extend their mercy on us. We all begged for forgiveness for we had transgressed against the deadly trio that was the law unto themselves.

After vain efforts of suppliant for clemency and after what seemed perpetuity of beseeching to the three, our prayers or rather pleas were answered or rather heeded. The trio that had instilled bouts of fear, as if on cue, let out a marathon raucous laughter consistent with some occult leaders from some West African country.

In unison, they piously as if in a trance and sacrifice to their gods, sunk their machetes into the belly of the earth, slicing it open, leaving the intestines bare and crimson. We all retreated into our shells with pounding hearts.

Having been satisfied with the effectiveness of their rituals, the trio marched to where the startled women waited in both awe and terror.

Yivhoni was savagely raped by Ndiringe as punishment for having resisted his advances.

On the break of dawn, we resumed with our journey to Wengezi where we intended to board buses to different destinations under the leadership of the menacing trio that then appeared relaxed and sexually spent.

I boarded the same vehicle with Yivhoni who was also Beitbridge bound. I was determined to settle in Johannesburg after being almost flushed out as a deserter by *Operation Gweja Dzoka Kumba.*

After alighting from a *malaitsha's* vehicle that had smuggled us into Johannesburg, we headed straight to a Methodist Church where some Zimbabweans had been offered sanctuary following the flaring up of xenophobic attacks in South Africa earlier that year of 2008.

Yivhoni and I were taken in together with a number of some desperate Zimbabweans who were fleeing from the country.

Together with Yivhoni, I would troop out of the sanctuary in search of menial jobs. Once the police or immigration officers swooped on us, we would produce asylum documents that entitled us to stay in that country. The documents enabled us to stay without being harassed by law enforcement and immigration officers. Most of those documents were fraudulently acquired.

Their holders would have told the South African Home Affairs department that they were under attack from State apparatus for their different political persuasions.

Three months down the line, Yivhoni was taken ill. She exhibited symptoms consistent with those of clinical malaria. She had also developed symptoms consistent with a sexual transmitted disease. After visiting a nearby clinic, she was confirmed to be three months pregnant.

She also tested HIV positive. She was treated for the sexually transmitted infection passed on to her by Ndiringe. Yivhoni wept uncontrollably.

She had at last conceived after more than a decade of futile attempts. It was because of her inability to conceive that had seen her husband marrying a second a wife. It was so sad.

CHAPTER 56

FLAMES OF HATE

As I panted and swept through the streets of Hillbrow that were lined with a plethora of barricades among them old tyres that drenched with petrol, food stuffs strewn all over desolated streets, blood tainted boulders and shattered vehicle wind screens, my heart skipped and leapt into my mouth with reckless abandon.

I could have swallowed it had I not been careful. I was glad that at least I had a heart to count on. As I wormed my way to a dark alley, something caught my attention. A stone's throw from where I stood transfixed, lay ashes of a human being.

A foreigner had been set ablaze by some overzealous South Africans who had blindly and drugged with heavy dosages of xenophobia, had responded to calls to crush foreigners who a vague and mysterious facebook character, *Vukani baZukulu baTshaka,* had said were worse off than frogs and toads.

That statement that was both rabble-rousing and full of vitriol incited violence among a few scoundrel, gullible and intolerant South Africans who had embraced the odium vocalizations, hook line and sinker. The few could be heard calling for the eviction of all foreigners whom they accused among other crimes of stealing their jobs.

Of contributing towards the economic render down that in turn had impacted on their social standings, of ruining amenities, of clinging to the largest economic cake in the running of shops, of committing petty crimes, of fueling crimes of passion, of lowering their living standards among a myriad of accusations.

As I drew closer to the burnt remains of somebody, a piece of cloth that had surprisingly survived the inferno. There was no need to call for a DNA forensic examination to determine the identity of the wretched alien of a drifter. A *vagrant* who had struggled to earn a living in a land of *stacks*. A *vagabond* whose shoes were lined with sparkling gems of gold.

That piece of cloth, a multi-coloured one belonged to Shorai Munakandafa who had made the traditional *jira reretso* stuff a part of him.

He used to comb for jobs on the streets of Hillbrow dangling that piece of cloth, a symbol of *mashave*.

He genuinely believed that that piece of cloth, that later turned out to be his identity document, could swing open breakthrough doors into his face. Times without number, he had landed some jobs, which he attributed to the piece of cloth. Shorai had died clutching his balls. Someone might have tugged at his privates before setting him alight with a tyre that dripped with petrol, a tyre that had been placed around his neck, a necklace of death. I wobbled to think of the piercing pain my countryman had gone through as firestorms of hate annihilated his body to the bone marrow.

I juddered to think of how Shorai's perpetrators felt as he wiggled, wriggled and writhed in pain as the flames of frustration pervaded into his body. Tears of frustration filled my eyes, tears of frustration meandered down my cheeks, tears of frustration trickled down my cheeks in a deluge of rivulets, rivulets of frustration, rivulets of anger, rivulets of sorrow and shame.

As I stood there weeping for my countryman, a tumult filtered into my ears from a distance. A man suddenly appeared from a blind alleyway sprinting at a breakneck speed with an armed and rowdy mob in hot pursuit.

The man appeared to have been bludgeoned by the blood thirst suckers of a mob as evidenced by his shirt that was saturated in blood. He rounded a bend, rode a tackle from a desperate pursuant and sold a dummy that left his pursuers chasing his shadow. The man swiftly slithered into a storm drain, which he turned into a makeshift sanctuary. He had made good his escape. His heart was pulsating threatening to rip the rib cage into smithereens. He piously prayed for his heart for he feared that the palpitations might give him away. He wondered whether his assailants who had been baying for his blood, his body and soul had ever been to church.

He wondered whether his aggressors had any shred of humanity left in them. He wondered whether some South Africans viewed themselves as Africans. He wondered what it was that had driven them to lynch some foreigners, plunder and pillage their fellow Africans.

He just could not believe that the South African government that reigned over a state that prided itself as a *Rainbow Nation* had failed to drive out the xenophobic ghost, a ghost that had now returned to haunt fellow Africans with nerve-jangling force and viciousness.

He strongly believed that departed Founding Fathers of the African Union must have been turning in their graves.

Surely, this was not the Africa that the Great Fathers, the iconic characters of the likes of Messrs' Julius *Mwalimu* Nyerere, Patrice Lumumba, Kwame Nkrumah and Emperor Haile Selassie had envisaged. Surely, they had every reason to turn in their graves with anger for their spirit of *ubuthu* and togetherness was under threat and siege. He wondered whether some South Africans were not foreigners somewhere and somehow. He wondered whether some South Africans were really superior to their fellow African brothers and sisters they had been hunting down the jungles of Soweto, Hillbrow, Durban and Johannesburg like wild animals. He wondered whether some South Africans still had conscience.

He wondered whether xenophobia was the biblical marked beast, a vampire that was prowling the streets of South Africa with serrated teeth that dripped with fresh blood. He appeared as if he were an *Alice in Wonderland* or rather *Allan in Wonderland.*

As he continued to wander in wonderland, he caught through the corner of his bruised eye, a South African rogue who had been part of his pursuers.

As he drew closer, Muchadura Marondamashanu, the Zimbabwean who was coiled in the storm drain closed his eyes to give his last prayer. The South African rogue was brandishing a machete that dripped with fresh blood.

In his left hand, he was clutching by plaited hair, the head of a Zimbabwean woman Ruramai who looked innocent and beautiful even in death. His pockets bulged with Ruramai's private parts and breasts. Her maimed torso was left to rot somewhere in an alley.

CHAPTER 57

SILHOUETTES OF DEATH

Muchadura never got to open his eyes again that night. He swiftly drifted into a land of nightmares that left him energy sapped and drenched to the bone. He never got to see the power of street lights illuminating their beams onto the streets. He never got to witness how lights on deserted streets would bath the streets with their beams of illuminations on the Illuminati.

He only got up after a tear gas canister that had been fired by the police to disperse some rowdy looters on the streets of Johannesburg, exploded into the storm drain, a drain that he had called home.

A drain that had offered him refugee when he appeared to have been walking in the shadows. A drain that had shielded him from the roving and prowling eye of a Zulu warrior who had marched past holding his conquest, his prey.

His prey dripped with blood, a prey that was created in God's own image, a prey that had never provoked him and a prey that had sought to eke an honest living far from Zimbabwe where the economy was shrinking by the day.

Before, everything seemed rosy. The grass had appeared greener. But once he had gone through the illegal route in which he had to waddle through the crocodile infested Limpopo River as well as weaving through marauding *umagumagumas*, he later realised that the pastures that he had left behind were greener and more luscious than those he had hoped for in the Rainbow Nation.

Back in Zimbabwe, Ruramai, a reputable hairdresser had walked out on her abusive, bed-hoping and irresponsible husband self-styled leader of a cult.

She had been in South Africa for the past five or so years where the hair dressing business had been roaring. Her success had rubbed onto her children whom she had managed to put through boarding schools.

The first one Nunurai was in her last semester at one of Zimbabwe's most revered and expensive private universities. She had managed to acquire a residential stand in a high-density area owned by one of Mutare's sprouting housing consortiums notorious for fleecing desperate housing seekers off their hard-earned cash.

When her estranged husband Terminator, got wind of his erstwhile wife's success, he sent a highly powered delegation to Ruramai's family with a view to broker a reconciliation.

Unfortunately, Ruramai who then was co-habiting with a Nigerian national, Okeke Okechukwu who was widely suspected to have been dabbling in narcotics and money laundering, spurned Terminator's overtures.

A fortnight had elapsed since Terminator who had jumped border into South Africa, had had a run in with Okeke in a Hillbrow restaurant. The bust up that had threatened to degenerate into a bloody skirmish, was quelled by the two rival suitors' friends.

Life threatening messages between the rival men, ran thick and fast. The very night Ruramai was beheaded, Okeke was said to have received a death threat from Terminator who was feared for his supernatural powers from the invisible spiritual realm.

The marauding Zulu warriors had swooped on Okeke and Ruramai as they were preparing to close shop for the day in the sprawling and crime torn settlement of Hillbrow.

When Okeke realised that they were under siege from the pillaging warriors, he shoved Ruramai into the passenger seat, thrust himself behind the wheel of his Rolls Royce, which was the envy of the Hillbrow community.

The Rolls Royce shot out of the parking bay onto the street as if from a catapult sending the warriors scurrying for cover. One of the warriors opened fire sending a barrage of bullets at the rocketing Rolls Royce.

Unfortunately, a stray bullet grazed Okeke's forehead resulting in a spray of blood that blinded his vision. With his vision blurred, Okechukwu ran into a barricade of refuse bins. Before Okeke could recollect, he was roughly bundled out. Another warrior hurled Ruramai out of the immaculate Rolls Royce and led her into a sanitary lane where a knoll of rubbish stood emitting tongues of foul shadows into the hood.

At the foot of the rubbish hillock, Ruramai's clothes were ripped apart before four machete-brandishing thugs who took turns to satisfy their sexual libidos on an alien who they wanted to purge savagely sexually assaulted her.

CHAPTER 58

THE UNHEEDED PLEA

Her pleas for mercy were ignored and hushed down with the sharpening of machetes on the walls of a dilapidated building that had suffered neglect for long.

As soon as the last rapist ejaculated into her honey jar, the first rapist to defile her, ordered her to say her last prayers whilst in a pious position. Instead of praying, Ruramai pleaded for the sparing of her life.

She even offered herself for another round of sexual assault. She wondered whether it was not the devilish work of the much-feared Mad Devirisher, a close buddy of Terminator, who was responsible for *mamhepo*, the winds that had engulfed her.

In wonderland, she felt the razor sharp sword slicing into her neck. She had no time to wail.

Only gurgles of blood gushed into the air leaving her assailants' clothes wet with crimson blood. Her attacker picked up her bloodied head, wiped blood from his cutlass with his tongue before ambling away with the head leaving the naked torso behind.

As soon as the ringleader walked away his walk of triumph, his subordinates descended heavily on Ruramai's torso, mutilating it in the process.

The cowards, the murderers lunged, lashed and mutilated her torso with all the power they could muster. As the torso still wondered, one of the trio poured petrol all over the naked torso before setting it on fire.

As Muchadura lay huddled in the tear smoke filled drain storm, he could faintly hear Ruramai's head wailing for her torso that had been engulfed with a blaze, a blaze that left her in a charred state.

Thusabantu the warrior who had taken pride in decapitating and parading of Ruramai's head which he intended to take to an informal settlement that housed foreigners among them Zimbabweans, was confronted by the police who challenged him to stop. Like an unhinged monster vampire, he charged towards the police who were armed to the teeth, threatening to hack their heads with his machete.

The police, who had been under instruction to quell their mutinous compatriots at all costs, opened fire razing him down to the ground.

As members of the law enforcement agents went down to retrieve Thusabantu's lifeless body, they stumbled upon Muchadura's body that had succumbed to the debilitating effects of tear smoke.

They picked him up too before bundling him into an ambulance that wheeled him to a nearby hospital where he was resuscitated and lived to tell tales of another day.

Three days after the gunning down of Thusabantu, police discovered Okeke's perforated body dumped at a dump site.

The body which was in an advanced state of decomposition, had eyes gorged out, manhood pulled out and tongue missing.

His hands and legs were tied with a barbed wire that left them perforated and lacerated. His metallic Rolls Royce, once the talk of his Hillbrow community had been reduced into a shell of metal after it was torched off.

After I spotted the rampaging machete wielding, knob carrying, wench and Okapi brandishing warriors coming after me, I sprinted to my heels. The rowdy warriors gave chase.

As the chasing and panting pack threatened to draw level, the Almighty handed me a baton stick that came with a fresh pair of sprinter's legs. I surged forward with lightning speed that left the chasing pack for dead and in bewilderment.

Another burst of speed saw me eating into a sewerage works area where ponds of human waste awaited treatment.

Having been satisfied with the progress I had made, I plunged into one of the hood's sewerage ponds that was filled to the neck with unctuous human waste. After what seemed like eternity, I emerged from the pool of pongs whiffing with odours. The self-styled warriors of madness were taken aback by my action. They stood with arms at akimbo hysterically laughing their lungs out. Before they knew it, I descended upon them with an avalanche of human excreta spraying them with a hail of bullets of smelly pooh as if I were Rambo. They abandoned their weapons and made a dash for freedom. Freedom from human faeces. Freedom from the clutches of a foreigner. Freedom from a foreigner whose freedom they had been curtailing.

I camouflaged myself with cakes of human faeces, fish and chips of human excreta as well as packets of greenish slimy, milky pooh. I had managed to break their pockets of resistance.

The warriors who had been angered by how I had out-sprinted and out-smarted them despite my handicap, went on a rampage, rummaging through the streets of Hillbrow in a desperate search for other foreigners. As they fled away from my sanctuary, their leader Musawenkosi signaled them to stop their flight. He believed that I would make good my escape. Sizabantu, his understudy, garbled something to the effect that there was need to surround the pond of pooh armed with some petrol bombs which they would hail at me from a distance. Musawenkosi ruthlessly shot down his suggestion.

Sibusiso too suggested that they poured petrol into the pond of pooh which they would set aflame. That suggestion too drew an onslaught of contemptuous comments from Musawenkosi who by then was heaving with anger. Musawenkosi strongly believed that there was no way I would allow them to come near the pond of pooh. I was determined to wage a war of pooh for my freedom. I was prepared to gun down for my life, which dangled in my own hands. I was just, but determined to fight for another day for my life was in my hands. Hands that were slimy, sticky and greenish with pooh. I was behaving like a lunatic street urchin who was out to protect his sanctuary, his space, his territory, his base or his station.

Musa called off the search party, removed the barrier off the pond of pongs as the warriors retired to other fertile hunting grounds. My heart sank when I heard the pattering feet of the warriors pattering and petering off from a distance. I had been saved by the grace of our gracious God.

www.ingramcontent.com/pod-product-compliance
Lightning Source LLC
Chambersburg PA
CBHW051829170626
46807CB00003B/1087